Cawl

Siôn Tomos Owen was born and raised first language Welsh in the Rhondda Valley. After a BA in Creative Writing and Media at Trinity College Carmarthen, Siôn won the Tudor Bevan Bursary Award in 2007, was runner up in the Terry Hetherington Young Writers Competition in 2014 and 2013 for short fiction, won the Young Writer's Prize in the Planet Essay Competition 2013 and was specially commended in the Welsh Poetry Competition 2014. His writing has been published in a number of magazines and anthologies including *Wales Arts Review*, *Ten of the Best*, *Square*, *Nu*, *Nu2*, *Planet*, *Red Poets* and *Cheval* and he's performed at many events including the Hay Literature Festival 2009–2014 and a very late night Poetry Slam on BBC Radio 5 live. He is the presenter of *Pobol y Rhondda* on S4C.

@sionmun
sionmun.tumblr.com

Cawl

Siôn Tomos Owen

PARTHIAN

Parthian, Cardigan SA43 1ED
www.parthianbooks.com
First published in 2016
© Siôn Tomos Owen 2016
ISBN 978-1-910901-52-6
Editor: Susie Wild
Cover images: Siôn Tomos Owen
Cover design by Robert Harries
Typeset by Elaine Sharples
Printed in EU by Pulsio SARL
Published with the financial support of the Welsh Books Council British
Library Cataloguing in Publication Data
A cataloguing record for this book is available from the British Library.

I Beckyboo ac Eira fach

and for my Rhondda, of course...

Contents

Mae Cymru

Through my calon
ac ar tip of fy tongues,
scales back the hanes
i ddenu'r two tafods,
nid fel machlud
a sunrise ond
dwy law 'all weithio
i atal bureaucracy
rhag choking
the living heulwen
allan o bilingualism
a chlymu cwlwm
yn eu windpipe.
Dyfal donc could dur
y ddwyieithrwydd
os ni gydiwyd
the bull by the curn
i coolio'r cicio gwyllt
a gadael y tarw a'r ddraig
to procreate
nid masturbate
bob gair mewn deddf
i osod the law
ar the door of the Senedd.

Running into the Ground

I run. I run 'cause it doesn't cost anything. Well, you might have to have a tidy pair of daps but apart from that you don't need nothing else. You don't have to buy equipment. You don't have to pay no cons. You just run. Pavements, roads, gullies, fields, tracks, trails, mountains, everywhere, anywhere. So long as you know how to come back. If you carry on running 'till you don't know how to come back, then you're buggered. You'll end up going nowhere, or worse, going round and round in circles. You'll wear yourself out and then even if you do find your way back, you'll be too knackered to try.

I always run there and back. Run all the way there and then come all the way back the same way. Same as the trains. Then I pass all the same things every day and I know exactly where I'm going. If anything changes, I'd know about it cause I'd see it changing bit-by-bit. I'd see it all as it was happening. The old things being knocked down and the new stuff going up. But I'd still remember what was there before. Like putting tracing paper over the top of it. Like I used to do when I was little, with the pictures in the newspaper. I'd draw me with my arm around the players in the team photo so it looked like I was there, or walking with all the other men on the way to work, or when they were all standing in the streets. I used to be a good drawer.

When I run, I never go round in a circle. I don't like not knowing what'll be in front of me. I couldn't do that, carry on going round until you ended up back where you started, without knowing how you got there. When I go somewhere and come back, I know exactly where I've been and how I've done it. Can't get surprised then. Can't get stopped by something in your way. Like, if they closed a road or knocked a bridge down. You'd have to find your way around and it might take ages 'till you did. Not that they'd knock a bridge down, unless it was dangerous or unsafe or something. Can't just go knocking bridges down for no reason and then not put another one up. There'd be no way over the river then would there? You'd be stuck. You wouldn't be able to cross without the bridge being there. Especially if it was rough, like when it rains.

There's only one bridge around here though, up to the colliery and that's been closed awhile. Hardly no one goes up there now, so I don't know if it'd matter that much if the bridge went...

If I do see people up there, by the colliery, they're just wandering round or standing on corners, waiting for something, or nothing, for anything. They just keep waiting for something to happen.

I see the same ones in the dole queue. They got the same expressions. Their waiting faces. But at least when you're in the queue, there's something at the end of it. 'Next.' At least there's some sort of destination, a purpose to stand there like a lemon, shuffling along. 'Okay, sign here and we'll see what we can find.' There's some sort of bastardised hope in the queue. 'No.' There's a collective hope. 'Still nothing, I'm afraid.' The bloke in front and the bloke behind are all hoping for the same thing. 'Sorry, we're not taking on.' The pot of gold at the end of the monochrome rainbow. 'Right, the van'll pick you up at 6.' Not even a pot really, a piece, a bloody penny would be worth it. 'Just don't get bloody caught. We ain't getting caught by the DWP for 'elpin' you out, right? If they catch you hobblin', we don't know nothin' 'bout you, you're on your own, butt.' So long as it was you who'd earned it.

But you can only stay in that queue so long. One way or another, something drives you out of it. Unless you've got the patience of a saint, there's only so much waiting a man can do before thoughts of anything other than waiting creeps in. Starts stirring in him. A hunger. Stirring like a pot of cawl. Only when you're waiting that long and smelling them lovely lamb and vegetable smells, you can feel it surging through you, warming you up. But when you lift that lid you find out the truth, that there's just a steaming pot of nothing underneath. Then that anger swells like a wave, the warm glow of optimism boiling over into hot scalding rage. But it's short-lived, as is such hope when you realise the situation and it ebbs away, pathetically... then you start begging them. Begging breeds survival, of society and your own sanity. You won't be long before begging turns to borrowing and soon you're stealing. Not pinching, but proper stealing. Either that or you'll go spare, off on one, doolally dap. Not a funny turn but a full-blown wobbly, where you don't know your arse from your elbow and you start screaming in the nights. It's hard to come back from that. Then you're on the slippery slope and when you live in a valley the slippery slopes are on both sides, and they all end up in the same place: Down. Down to the city.

The irony of it. We used to feed them and now we need them to feed us. The industrial revolution made us kings. Doing a job of worth, fuelling the world with our hands and trams and picks. We fired up the world's industries from the black belly of this valley. Not just this valley, but the whole of the South Wales coalfield, but we played our part. Up until that last tram was sent out, we worked with spit and sinew for our worth... now look at us. Those trains were laden with our labours, travelling down through the villages and towns, to the stations and ports and sent out to the world!

Now we fill those trains like cattle, equally laden. To work away. Paid to leave and paying to come home. Only some know they'll keep returning, while others come back up like that last tram, knowing they won't be going back down. Redundant. Unnecessary. Useless to you. You've got to be callous to tell a man that to his face. To render him redundant is to throw a shovel into his chest and dig out his heart. A man's being is his work. Take that away and there's not much left but blood and bone.

We're born for work. We're built for it. Our muscles made for building and digging and burning our own energy to serve our own purpose. The dirt beneath our nails, proof of our existence. Many a man down the pit had superstitions of not washing his back for it would wash away his strength, like a river would wear down the rocks. But I had superstitions about the dirt beneath my nails. To see them scrubbed clean was to scour the past from my very hands. I didn't want to dirty my future by washing away the past. A man who does not know his history is doomed to repeat it.

If my arms ached, it was because I knew I'd worked hard the day before. A sign of a good day's work. An echo for the day to come. A smile would find its way to my lips like a pocket of air to the surface of a lake, rippling with the pain and pride of a thousand men. I haven't heard that echo since that final day. The pride has drained away. The pain remains.

I run and I run and I run to burn my lungs and try to find the fire that once fuelled me. But I can't bloody find it. It's not the same fire that burns. It hurts like hell but it's not the same. That aching sensation, the satisfaction in my arms and my back and my legs. Knowing that everything I did, I deserved to do. Every scrap of food I ate and every pint I drank, I had earned in sweat down with the rest of them. I had a place in the world. I was a part of the great machinery of men. I belonged in that hole. Not in this one. This is far blacker and darker than any shaft. At least down there I knew where to go to get out, where to turn for light, to come up for air, to find the sun on my face, for the wind to blow away the dust. But here, where I am now, this is closer to hell than any depth I ever worked.

My mother's begun to notice.

'You alright? Small you've gone. What's the matter with you? You eating tidy?' she asked while peeling spuds into a pan in the lean-to kitchen at the back of the house.

'I'm just running, Mam.'

'But there's nothing to you.'

'Running he is, mun,' shouted my father. My mother frowned at him through the old window that looked into the living room. He didn't need to shout, you could whisper in the front room and hear it in the kitchen. Two up two down terraces ain't built for secrets, not for lack of trying.

'I'm just running more than usual, that's all, Mam,' I said.

'It's not normal to run like that. People will think you're running from something,' she said, narrowing her eyes at me. 'A man needs to eat too,' she walked into the living room and placed a plate of enough before me as I sat next to my father at the wooden fold-out table.

'I am eating, Mam,' I said staring at the plate.

'He is eating, gel, stop fussing,' said Dad. 'Even if he wasn't, you'd make sure of it any- how. Look at the size of that plate! More than my last two meals!'

My mother furrowed her brow and eyed me up and down again before returning to the kitchen.

'Have half of this with me now, Dad,' I said, gesturing quietly so my mother wouldn't hear.

'Don't be so soft...' he said before breaking into a violent coughing fit. Bad enough to make my mother stop briefly, to listen, to make sure.

'You keep running,' he said once he'd caught his breath again, wiping his mouth with his hanky. 'No need to be daft like this, you know what she's like.' His eyes looking down at his hanky, checking. Slowly being beaten up from the inside.

'Where d'you run to last?' he asked.

'Same place,' I said. 'Up top.'

He shook his head. 'You shouldn't, mun. What good's that doing?' The same old argument.

'Ain't that many places I can go without ending up there, Dad. The town was built around it. All roads lead to Rome.'

'Rome was sacked.'

'So were we,' I said, trying not to take the bait. 'It's just the way I go, Dad.'

'Is it hell. Stop obsessing over it. No need for it, mun. It's not sleeping. Dead it is. It's gone! They won't start it back up!'

'I know that. I'm not stupid.'

'Leave it be, then.'

My mother brought in my father's plate and placed her own down on the wicker placemat. She had cut up his food into small pieces again. I caught the look he gave her.

'It's not doing no one no harm is it? What am I doing if not learning from the mistakes?' I asked.

'What bloody mistakes?'

'You know what I'm on about.'

'Do we have to do this again?' my mother pleaded.

'Ush now!' my father told her. 'There were no mistakes. Hundreds had closed before all that nonsense with her and the strikes. Things pack in. You can't go digging the hell out of something forever. You end up leaving it hollow.'

'Like a tomb.' My mother almost whispered, but still the emphasis rang out around the table, 'men only ever dig holes that deep for greed and graves.'

'They would have cut their losses and built a bloody iron cross on the pithead as a parting shot!' I immediately regretted my words.

'Now you watch your mouth!' My father thundered quietly, pointing his enormous misshapen finger at me from the chair, his eyes ablaze.

'Sorry, Dad.'

'Ceri'd be more than glad they closed it. He'd have closed every one if he could have but he ended up having no choice but to work down there and what bloody good did that do him?' He asked, slamming the table.

My mother picked up her plate and left the table for the front room.

'Mam...' I chased her with my words. My father watched her leave.

'He's still up there— in there somewhere and he never even wanted to go in! He had no bastard choice and here you are, after getting out of there in one piece and you want to go back down?' My father clasped his forehead, and leaned over onto the table, shaking his head at memories he wanted gone.

I sat, silently repeating the same argument with myself. My father knew too well the cost it had on us locally when it closed but his history with mining was stained heavily with death. His father, two brothers and his firstborn. I was a casualty of circumstance but to my father, I was a living casualty, at least.

My brother hated it, to the point of fighting to keep me from there, beating up friends who jostled me for staying on at school and not joining them. He always thought I wanted to be like him, but that wasn't it. It wasn't that I wanted to follow him, as he did my father, and his father before him. There was no need for me to go but I chose to. It was the way he was received when he was walking home. The way people looked at him and the way that he would look back. It was a mutual respect that I would only see in that walk home, black-faced and determined. No briefcase or posh car ever got those same looks.

Dad wasn't as he was now, he was done with the pit by then but whereas I saw pride in his face when Ceri caused to come home, I was too naive to understand it. I went for me, not for tradition but for a sense of worth. For something that I hoped would reflect in his eyes. But my father's look was different, but I couldn't see it then. What I saw was pride in the work Ceri did, not my father's daily concern until his son returned from a place that forged memories in his hardened lungs. Memories that would collapse under the weight of regret that choked my father's throat and mutilated my mother's grief.

It changed after the accident. Lots changes after accidents, especially ones in small towns like this one. When I decided to go, It wasn't pride I saw on their faces as I walked home that day, but relief. I didn't want bloody relief! I wanted them to look and see me walking home and give me the same nods and we'd have the same silent exchanges of 'Well done, butt. You're doing it'. But they didn't. They heard my father's rants and my mother's tears at the choice I made.

My father then, much like the village, wasn't watching Ceri coming back from work, he was seeing him returning home, safe, unbroken.

Then they began seeing me leave for work but it was Ceri they saw walking home and heartbreak would shake their heads at the memory. The ones that did see me, gave me the 'never mind' wink, as if I had no choice but to continue the work like some familiar production line. But I had the choice and I chose to go in. It's what I wanted to do. It wasn't a mantle handed down to me, that I was obliged to carry on the work. I did it for me. Then they went and bloody took it away! They took it all away. The striving and the pride and the worth that came with it, they took that and all. The hope of seeing those looks left when they shut those gates.

There was no nostalgia for it, no longing, only anger after the pit closed. Those 'never mind' winks were constant from then on. And they devoured me. They were sympathetic at first when we passed. But when more pits closed and we continued to pass, in clean clothes, in the middle of the day, without that familiar gait of toil and triumph, but of misery and an unfulfilled day, then came pity. Their half smiles were devastating, their pats on the back, crippling. The brutal irony of Ceri's life, crushed in the darkness, gasping for life. Those constant looks of pity in the daylight were what was slowly suffocating me. Like my father, I was battling with a raging illness that was killing me from the inside.

'I just want to go back to work, Dad,' I tried. 'It's all I know.'

'Your brother should have been a lesson learned and you still went,' he said, slowly lifting his gaze. 'I'm sitting here coughing my bastard guts up and you still wen...'

As if for effect, he erupted into a coughing fit, wheezing red-faced, like he was continuing the argument in a language I didn't understand. A language of consequence and sacrifice. A language my father was fluent in.

I put my hand out to steady him in his chair. Exhausted, he slouched back and tilted his head to look at me, his eyes wet.

'Leave it be, now,' he said. 'Leave it be.'

I have this dream where I'm running up the top end of the valley. I usually run early in the morning when it's coldest and your breath is white and puffing like an engine. But in this dream it's too dark for me to see anything tidy and I keep going the wrong way, finding myself up in dead ends. It's hot, muggy, like the bowels of the earth and I'm pouring with sweat but my breath is still swirling until it's all around me. I can't see anything, but I'm still running. Then I can hear the flap-flap of someone else running behind me. I turn around to look but I can't see anyone, so I keep running. It feels like a clock in an empty room. The second hand catching up with the minutes, moving closer all the time. It gets nearer and nearer, getting louder and louder like the pistons of a train, until I can see who it is. It's me.

It's me, coming out of my own swirling breath. But it's not me. I'm so thin that it looks like I shouldn't be able to run. My skin is pale and grey, almost see-through, like a new-born fish. My eyes are bulging out of my head, glazed, not looking at anything, just staring ahead. He – it – is running right behind me. It doesn't try to go around me. It doesn't want to go around me. It's trying to get *into* me, so it can *be* me. So I run harder but it doesn't make any difference. It just keeps running and running and running and getting closer and closer. I'm gasping for air and it's so hot that I start struggling to keep my pace and I know that when it gets to me I'm going to stop running and it's going to stop running. Then we'll both just stop. I'll just stop dead. Then there won't be a me anymore. It'll just be this pale, skinny, dead me, not running, just standing, doing nothing, and when that happens, I might as well be dead. When that happens I will be dead.

Batman (1989)

It's raining
And I'm wet.
It's odd.
I don't remember rain from my childhood.
Not at all.
I know it must have rained
Because I remember my coat.
I remember being Batman.
I remember running around with just my hood on,
Being Batman.
Batman never did much
But run around with his hood on,
His coat flapping behind him like a cape.
I remember being Batman
And lots of queues.
Dad was Robin
Standing in the queue.
I wanted him to be Superman
But he said he couldn't be Superman.
Not when he was in the queue.
He said he'd be Superman
When he didn't have to be in the queue anymore.
When he was in the queue,

He was Robin.

Dad was Robin

Long after I'd stopped being Batman.

Long after I outgrew my coat.

Write About What You Know (In Praise of a Valley)

After Rhydwen Williams

Rhondda!
    This patient valley
Though ebullient under relentless skies,
Its remaining limbs,
Trehafod to Blaen-cwm
Llwyncelyn to Maerdy –
Straining, an exhausted mother
Continuing to conceive, in her advancing years.
Here, frontiers of new forestry
Hide the heaped fossils of the forgotten,
Tall unused stacks—
Tired, untold stories—
Seeping from the mortar and stone
Of those old workhorses
Who defied the iron whore;
Here, skulls underground
Remain, long lost eyes
And voices – a people's past
Trickling like a residue
Through discarded plastic flagons and BBQs.
Here, where sloshing mountain streams
Scar the mountain wet and white

From the torrents we receive,

An economic haemorrhage,

After industry's rape and abandonment –

Only moonscaped hills' replanted memory can conceal.

Once upon our past,

Walls of black gold and wooden prop

In dry-lung huddles in the hills,

An offering of work or mercy

On the hungry sons and giddy aunts;

Night owls and morning bells

Started the slopes,

As unrelenting to the mourner's ears.

The immeasurable loss;

Here too, slag and boulders

Sparred with purple heather, foxglove and fern,

The unchanged winds

Splashed colour back into the trees...

The last hooter bore the night

Blacker than a miner's throat,

And the wheels of the daft and idle

Reprieved the dusk of

The male voice choir's song!

That woman said, 'Let there be dark times'
And there were dark times.
The last pit;
The darkness deflowered the field,
Broke its back,
Embraced the old virgin's final quiver.
Here, man cratered his world,
Terraces, straight, taut, like leashes
Around the necks of dogs
Huddled up to their God's houses,
Llys Bethel, Ty Tabernacl, Llys Moriah, Ty Noddfa, Llys Siloh,
Where sparrows found a bite,
The saints, a sanitary room,
The sinner, a lonely haven.

It is a saga tomorrow has already forgotten,
The jellied stones are meek
And the mountains still 'share',
Proud yet devoured by
Their 'Green' judgment
From the sealed corridors of The Bay,
They vet Pentre, Ystrad, Ferndale, Treorchy, Blaencwm.
Where ghosts of men and lorries
Move above the rattle of yesterday's trams
And the din of the whirling, wind-driven blades...

Come on 'en! See where the weed now roams,
The pissheads rant
Their obscene parabling for powder
And ounces of green.
See where the bars were burnt
As door to door
Poured out the corpses
At The Banc's feet,
And the 'lush' women,
Appalled, barebacked and pregnant,
Overwhelmed the valley
With a tidal sheath!

'Good Grief,' said the television
Peering over the pulpit
Like vultures circling – it was
The day they buried young Maerdy,
Mangled under the fall.
'Good riddance to the bitterest fruit,
Plucked before the tree was felled.
Yet heed their cores,
Inside there are gallstones
Passed as a nugget of coal,
Planted in the hearth it will glow and glow
Into an ember of resentment
For the future...'

And all the unions and the committee members said, Amen.

And it came to pass
Siblings idle, muscles rusting,
Muffled colliers, hunger, parched
Found tips in taverns,
Spoke English now, thankless.
Gusty 'Wales this week' voices
Singing before the shutters.
Park and Dare to Downing Street
For a jobseeker's coin and Maggie's bite,
Scouring for a smile –
'Not today', 'Thenkiw', 'Nothing today', 'Thenkiw'.
They went away –
Singing songs they do not understand
'Mya glower dinner lice
In Gall who hung navy...'
And all the 'oh dear's and 'dur's,
Knells and bolted doors,
Precious kids and knock-kneed teens
Vegetated...
As though anger
Had escaped out of Parliament – via Pontypridd
For a trouncing
Up the Taff.

Back in the valley.

The remaining wives and mothers

Needed to scrimp and save

In lean-to kitchens,

Stirred their empty pots

As the men spent more time in allotments.

Passing time like a small boy's troubles,

Ribbing each other for their long hair

And drank the valleys champagne dry

Before swearing – just for a lark –

To curse the last train as it leaves!

Aye, but it needed more than Luciana's frothy coffees...

She never missed a thing,

From irrepressible little bird's tales, beaten wives and

'Who-do-you-think's-having-who's-baby-again?'

To fight the stagnation that was settling in.

Those small boy's troubles maintained,

They outgrew their peace and love and long hair,

Grew a tash like Freddie Mercury,

But then took away his work clothes and clipped his wings,

His future dark like Stevie Nicks' brooding eyes

And the DWP came along... and gave them benefits

(but not of the doubt).

Clipped wings and benefits!
The valley was never the same.

Who was to know
That to discard the workforce,
The economic curfew and the nurtured smile,
The cruel stipulates – domiciled beneath us –
The chicken-shit gorse, snaking the ravaged fields,
Would inevitably lead to;
>   Fire and water battling from summer teens,
>   Dust on the sons thrust into the social line,
>   Suicides withstanding, still scandals in the choir,
>   The piano's under lock and key, the TV's on the mantlepiece,
>   The pictures of the town before, on walls to remember who we were,
>   The baby in the back garden with the bathwater around it,
>   Silence in the mobile phone and noise from the car,
>   Hands always on their organ or reaching for a tit,
>   The paedophile up the mountain, not the stranger in the Co-op,
>   The names on the cenotaph and the children pissing in the park...
>   And the old language
>   On a young boy's lips
>   Struggling to converse
>   With his own generation?

Boy,

You scrambler in the Llanwonno wind,

A mangled mother-bred,

Ready for 'The Comp',

Over the future's clusterfuck scratchcard,

Something new departing in your eyes,

A career defaced,

Your father and grandfather

Cowed:

Now where they lie,

Shunted into the sideshow of the tourists' eye,

A cemented silence,

Tells of their powerlessness...

Cwmparc to Cardiff Gate, Clydach to Cathays,

They, who were belligerent to your body,

Succumbed into welcoming new customers

To those call centres

But the muzak never snatched you from

The retired screams of Pentwyn

Nor the social stereotypes' stranglehold of Penrhys.

Girl,

You with your morning smile

And your many eyes,

Listen, listen,

While tomorrow waits

For your well-worn breasts

And the recycled stencil of your bones,

To forgo another brood,

With an old, old line,

As effulgent as streetlight neons,

Witness the second coming,

Of forgoing our feelings,

Reaping the benefits of

Shitting on us natives, once more,

On the valley that was killed

And left to rise again,

Incorrigible like it is...

Oh, Christ...

26

Estate of Mind: Gurnos

Nature named
nurture maimed
stereotypecast
faster than you can say
estate, in a state, a spate
of new opposite the old
clean slate, replaced
by green space
slow-paced, recovery...
Abandoned vehicles
tickle the ventricles of public walkways
Driven away, working away,
all the while weakened if they stay
Under grey skies
and high-rise hospitals
named after royalty
in line,
waiting just as long,
God don't save the wrong sort
cavorting along the
branches of oak, poplar, yew
spread among the
lavender, heather, honeysuckle

bare-knuckle matchstick men remembering,

rendering bygones as forgone concrete conclusions,

illusions of hell-on-earth painted by headlines

on breadlines, kneads lies

from statistics

misquoted and coated in reputations

raised above Crawshay's stone

cold callousness

betraying and baying for blood

through history books

and revolution's nooks and crannies,

get outs and get in and Dic Penderyns

from castles to cattle grids

skid marks across cast-ironworked resolutions

through the years and viaducts

via those who stuck to their guns and their homes

to become the residents, the inhabitants

the have and have nots,

the cots, the cribs, the cradles,

the ladles that stir the lives

of husbands, wives, children

steered in their own direction,

forging their own image

of fears and fire, friends and funerals,

in their own reflection,

a collection of everything
but inverted commas
placed around the necks of
the next '3G Generation'.

Confounded by Definition

A noun's a broken ladder
if working's how we live.
Since the middle and the upper
are both adjectives.

The dictionary describes
an adjective as 'dependant'
so is the working class prescribed
as 'providing for', expectant?

If working's the objective
to climbing to the middle,
the truth? It's a subjunctive:
the upper is a fiddle.

'The upper hand's an idiom,
'not deducible alone'.
Without the other words they're... um,
useless, idle, prone.

So if the upper's merely lurking
let the editing begin!
Since the lower and the working
are sardonic synonyms.

The irony's abundant
that an 'action' cannot curb,
to 'become redundant',
cruelly, is a verb.

Hello,
I'm Eric
Pickles.

©SIÔNMUN

42

Revolootion

By incubating poverty you force them to the streets.
In anger, they inevitably aim their rages at the police.
Doing nothing but increasing
the beast that is growing
and throwing bricks and stones,
breaking the bones of communities,
since there's no longer local amenities.

These days are blacker than the PM sees
from his quiet villa in Tuscany.
Avoiding the Ultra Violent UV
behind his chianti and antipasti.
Applying the rhetoric up to factor fifty
to soothe the simmering skin of Britain,
cracking and burning under its neon nightmare
of said 'socioeconomic disease'.
Just relax as London's brought to its knees
'People, please! You're The Big Society!
I'll condemn the riots on the BBC,
if you wait till I'm back from Arrivals, at least.'

Business or pleasure or necessity?
Now it's time to confess that these incidents
Are the result of public unease.
This mess, Theresa, doesn't stem
From Facebook or Twitter or BBM,
But from the hook, line & bitterness,
From a lack of political interest,
In keeping the upper classes close to your chest.

With the 'squeezed middle', you've been doing your best
But the out-of-work(ing) classes are fed up!
As it's finally leaked how morally corrupt
Your courting of Murdoch's media's been,
As you hide behind your heckles of branding them obscene,
you rush to tar corruption with the same reforming brush
the law becomes uncouth, deforming the truth
by crushing the facts to rubble and dust
As communities burn and relationships rust.

You hush-hush the shame and pity that pockmarks the capital city,
Who disagree with You & Yours.
Count the fatalities as Me & Mine mentalities take things
into their own hands, into their own vans filled with top brands
and a couple of grands worth of plasmas.
While you watch the unfolding drama on rolling news.

Shame on you,

this could have been dealt with in time,

If you hadn't cut 25% of 999.

Don't label these as class-rioting events,

Tottenham, North London was fuelled by one incident.

Thursday 06:46, a black cab stood parked.

All it took was a bullet. All it took was a spark.

Armed officers, a father of four and a question mark.

©SIÔNMUN

Cuts

I cut myself.

I cut myself to help the economy.
When I draw the smallest slit
in the purse of my groin,
I know that these cuts will reduce
the deficit.

Trickle-down economics
from the banks
of my knees
into the red
pool at my feet.

I cut myself to help
the razor and plaster industries.

I don't need A & E
because this is private.
Between you and me—
I know
these cuts are helping
everyone.

I've got the scars to prove it.

Wales in Hard Times
The Poet, The Donkey and The Quandary: A Quest to Understand the Political Landscape of the Valleys during a Global Economic Crisis

At the time of the 2010 UK elections, in the immediate aftermath of a recession, I was a poet. The manufacturing company I had worked at for almost two years went into administration and I was made redundant, after which I settled on 'Poet' rather than calling myself 'unemployed' or 'between jobs'. If my sixteen-year-old artistically-minded self had seen me in my previous job, sitting in an office, studying tenders and punching numbers into a computer spreadsheet he would have sharpened his paintbrush and committed hara-kiri. It wasn't a job that I was particularly fond of but one that I learned a great deal from. I had mainly worked in shops, warehouses and building sites, and the replacement of site banter with office politics was an eye-opener, a fist-clencher and back-stabber. It was an average March morning when a stream of dark-suited men stormed into the office unannounced and told us to close everything down. After two days in administrative limbo I was freed from my desk job to explore other avenues of employment. As the weeks wore on, those avenues increasingly became marked with 'No entry' signs. The eminent Rhondda author, Gwyn Thomas, wrote that, 'The beauty is in the walking – we are betrayed by destinations'. How right he was about the months to follow. The destinations were definitely betraying me, but the walking...

To add routine to the monotony of an unemployed day, I began reading the papers thoroughly. Weeks turned into months of applying for any job from window cleaner to media worker (telesales) and hearing nothing back. I was a frustrated 'over-skilled', underemployed advert for Generation Y. A generation of algae on the surface of a reservoir of promised opportunity that was being dredged by the recession. So, as my grandfathers did in such times in the workmen's halls and libraries that they had built for themselves, I began to educate myself. I read the *Western Mail* that my parents had delivered to the house, then the *Guardian* online. I'd fetch *The Independent* from the newsagents, read *The Week* and *Prospect* in the library – anything I could get my hands on. I was devouring current affairs faster than a politician could avoid a question, and I slowly began to learn how and why they did it too.

I hadn't been particularly politically-minded until this point, but my father had always said, given the right circumstances, I would eventually become so. However, at university I had been on marches over rising student fees and my picture had turned up on a website declaring me a 'Red Socialist', which I only later found out was meant to be an insult. Coming from an ex-coal mining valley community, the ideological implications of socialism were ingrained in me, but the concept of socialism as something to fear or avoid was something alien that had to be explained to me by an American Studies lecturer. I was perplexed by how it could be viewed as a bad thing until he explained that these views were historically driven by socialism's links to America's complicated and fantastical relationship with communist countries, and the negative connotations socialism had in thwarting 'democracy' and, inevitably, the true American Dream of capitalism. It was a revelation of the wider world to an intrigued Valley boy.

By April 2010, the three-way televised election debates were underway. I was pretty clued up on what primary colour the party leaders were as well as which yarn each one was spinning: Anti-Blairite, Post-Thatcherite, Neo-Gladstonite. These debates would prove the tipping point for the Liberal-Democrats and echo in the dawn of Cleggmania. This was the phrase coined by the media after the public's hope swelled on seeing a political leader who seemed to offer something new: honesty. Polls screamed that we'd vote in hordes for the new Messiah (only 23% voted with *actual* ballot papers, not superlatives), yet it took less than a year to discover that yellow-tie man was just another very naughty boy and the novelty of his honest approach was neo-bullshitism.

By this point I had also watched Series Three of *The Wire*. This is *the* 'Politics' series and follows the Mayoral Campaign of Tommy Carcetti as the social background to the ongoing drug-running turf wars on the streets of Baltimore. I'm not ashamed to say that I learned and understood more about the intricacies of politics from those 14 episodes than in all the articles, columns and Oxford Short Introductions I'd read *trying* to understand it.

My poetry became fuelled by my new-found interest in the ever-present issue of politics, and I had found a platform on Facebook and Twitter which served to start debates, rather than scrolling 50 photos of old school friends' new babies, or statuses washing dirty laundry in public. I had folders (physical and digital) full of social commentary poems and an iPod full of political podcasts. I was immersed in and riveted by it all.

Conservatives to Re-open the Mines: A Dialogue

'Reopen the mines!
(For out of sight out of mind)
Numb our oldest feud.'

'Unclose the mines.
This valley's made for churning
Our souls for the flue.'

'Re-export the coal.
Striking into the earth's core.
Fibres of your being.'

'Re-expose the cuts.
Blue veins black. Comrades of dust,
In darkness, living.'

'Revisit the face.
Fire up enthusiasms:
The furnace of change!'

'Envisage our face.
Fire and pick and white-eyed.
Black marks on a page.'

The power to rule the people inevitably corrupts politicians worldwide. The only difference is that in democratically elected nations, which uphold the Western Utopia of Governance that we so wish to impose on the rest of the world, the corruption is far more discreet. It's managed, polished, repackaged, ingested and repeated so that all we are left with is the old adage: 'All politicians are liars and are all in it for themselves,' and we leave it at that.

When I first voted in the local elections in 2004, after turning 18, when I had yet to immerse myself in politics, I voted for the only person on the ballot that I had heard of. I knew him, I knew he was local to the area and I knew he was a good man. I would see him walking around town, I would speak to him and later he would tutor me during my A levels. It just so happened that he was the ward member for Plaid Cymru. That year they retained the Treorchy ward and so I assumed that I had made the right call based on the collective vote of my community.

Four years later I was a student at Trinity College Carmarthen, and out of discord with the war in Iraq, a number of my friends voted for the Liberal Democrats (stereotypically, the Lib Dems being the so-called left-leaning voice of the student). Since I had no idea who the candidates were, I voted Plaid again because I felt I had voted 'correctly' the previous time. They also won in Carmarthen. It seems I was on a roll.

When I returned home, while speaking to some older voters in a Brachi's cafe about the election, I mentioned how I had voted. They were appalled at my reasoning. What I deemed a logical extension of my naive political apathy enraged them. Why hadn't I taken into account any current affairs or read up on anything before casting my vote? I was considered a brazen fool for even mentioning it to them.

At the time I took it on the chin. Then I asked them who *they* voted for and why. Almost all replied 'Labour' and I noted it as my first encounter with party differences.

What I assumed would be a simple exchange became much more confusing, and what followed stymied genuine political discussion: 'My father voted Labour and his father and his before that and I *always* will, don't matter who the guy is.'

This wouldn't be the last time I'd hear this. But it started to make me question things about my beloved valley and its people that I hadn't before. The old joke that if you pinned a red lapel on a donkey in the Rhondda, people would vote for it, was actually true! Strong, opinionated people who stood up for what was right no matter who the oppressor was, began to seem like... sheep. I couldn't handle another stereotype.

By 2010, the shit-storm that was the global economic crisis was raging, the lies about WMDs in Iraq had been exposed, Brown had replaced Blair as prime minister and politicians had been exposed for exploiting their expenses. Even the most fervent member of the Labour Party, I thought, must have been questioning their government. Now armed with understanding on the subjects along with my own informed views, I could *actually* hold discussions and debates with those people who had berated my choices last time around.

I was now in a quandary as to my own political leanings from information overload and discussions with canvassers. I wanted to make an informed choice and so needed this platform to hash out the pros and cons, the local and national debates that I assumed took place in the pubs and clubs during elections. But, alas, where I believed a new dialogue could be forged from the flames of five years of controversies and economic collapse, their opinions remained bafflingly stagnant.

I was again chastised by the Brachi's regulars for questioning their resolve. They saw it as political heritage whereas I saw it as nostalgic ignorance. The 'issues' would not cloud their judgment. There are two options: Labour or Conservative. Red or Blue, it was black and white to them. I mentioned the Lib Dems or Plaid Cymru, but they assured

me that locally or nationally there was no grey area. Where I saw a rainbow of options they saw two opposing ends. I was confused by the simplicity of their argument and gutted by what I saw as bigotry in my fellow comrades.

What made things worse was that I was made to feel the naive fool, again, come election day, as I was ensconced by the middle ground. On telly the posh boy and the old guard exchanged repeated barbs of yore as the pale new rider who spoke of clarity and change convinced my mark upon the ballot.

I voted Lib-Dem.

But all it took was five days of rolling news for me to regret my decision. It took even less time for those I considered foolish with antiquated views to don their armour and lay into me for what seemed to them to be geo-political treason: 'Look what you've gone and done now! You with your bloody hippy views to try to change things and look what's bloody happened!'

I genuinely felt to blame, since I truly believed I could skew the pendulum, change the platform, but all I did was play into the hands of my Labour-voting neighbours for argument's sake. Where I thought they were cutting off their noses to spite their faces, what they were actually doing was making sure the scars were visible. But these scars were not new, as I would learn from the death of an old woman a few years later.

On the 8th of April 2013, Margaret Thatcher died. I then saw first-hand what I struggled to comprehend during those early experiences of drawing party lines and fathoming political ideals. I knew 'that woman' was not a friend of these parts and that many considered her *the* enemy. But being born the same year as the great miners' strike I was told by 'moderates' that I 'had no right' to voice my disapproving opinions of her since I was 'far too young to remember' let alone understand those times. I realised that the arguments of 'Thatcher's Children' here in the Rhondda are based on an ideology rather than being the uneducated opinions of those too young to witness her policies. I may not have understood what was happening at the time but I can now see and understand what has happened since.

The economic scars left here are still fresh. There isn't a single mine open (Maerdy was the last to close in 1990), very few factories are left (Burberry's closed in 2007), and we haemorrhage down the railway line to Cardiff more and more to work in call centres: the mineshafts of the age. Nothing is made here anymore. We fuelled the world and now we are the burned-out embers of a forgotten industry which has been replaced by derelict chimney stacks, rusting trams on motocross-gouged tips, and crumbling factory warehouses where I used to aim to smash the glass on the top floor windows. Oh, the shattering of metaphorical irony.

Walking past the old EMI factory in Treorchy, which has stood ruined for almost a decade now, the level of economic desperation and need hits home. There are plans to open a new Tesco on this site. Plans that have been in the pipeline for years but have come up against opposition. It may ruin the nature of the town and will definitely create traffic congestion but it would also fill a gaping chasm of youth unemployment in the area.

Those Labour stalwarts were not so because they were driven by Blair, Brown or Miliband's policies but rather they were opposed to returning to a time where they were driven by Thatcher's. The political landscape has changed radically, metamorphosed into a situation where politicians are not only the governors of the land but are the celebrities of television, radio, Facebook and Twitter. With even more ways to connect to the electorate, modern politicians seem so far away from the times when my sparring partners' opinions were formed. There is a fear and an anger and a sense of hopeless-ness that permeates through their staunch dedication to *their* party. They've lived through a time where everything changed, and the phrase 'those who do not know their history are doomed to repeat it' remains fresh. Thankfully this ideology remains ingrained in some, who are impassioned enough to voice those opinions and not be quelled by the 'respect the dead' nonsense spouted on social media as a way of damp-ening free speech. A frail old woman Thatcher may have been, but in 2013 she was staying at The Ritz, London, surrounded by luxury, as we suffer austerity and hardship, surrounded by the remnants of a dying community, industry and society.

What I'm still learning is that come the next election there may be a bitter pill to swallow if I am to truly understand how politics works around here and how it genuinely affects us as a valley, a county and a country. Yet the grand irony of all this is that during these quarrelsome, grassroots debates in the heart of the South Wales valleys, the Welsh Assembly was hardly even mentioned.

The stone from which our blood is drawn

Remembering is a trust
of stone and song and complaining,
moaning and groaning and singing
in full voice
and in silence,
in yesterday's rain,
in puddles that sit, reflecting
and protecting today's
'Clouds around our heart.'
At anyone who wishes
to look down into tomorrow
and be soaked, elevated and evaporated
into a *hiraeth* of heritage.
Bones that were borrowed from hallowed hills
gave birth to us as well as killed
in mourning and in metaphor.

These doors to the workmen's halls,
reference libraries
and quarries of collected memories
are hinged
to the present, who don their tribal armour
of struggle

and smile against the stereotypes
piped through to the outside subconscious,
by sleight of hand and slip of eye.
The other side of these narrow hills,
(That mean the world to us)
are just the cusp of greater things
within the melting pot
that we still stir:

The cawl of culture

that warms the collective cockles of our hearts.
The bridge between before and yet-to-be
needs rebuilding or the burning will continue.
The cycle of creation keeps turning,
the circle of belonging keeps yearning
for 'when we used to',
refusing to let it drop,
tugging on hopeless heartstrings
while the trains keep departing,
carting the workhorses
to their equivalent workhouses.

We need kick-starting,
keep laughing, as the population is halving.

we are a burgeoning movement.
An amalgam of migration,
thrust into situations that forged nations
trusted to hollow the creations
that would define us,
and deny us
while it lined us up.
A flight of feet filling the streets,
milking the teat of the terraces,
transforming mere mountains
into memories, malleable monuments
and moments bubbling to the surface.
We're performing a service to ourselves.

The New Rhondda Revolution!
We are an evolution,
an embryonic community.
These peaks and troughs
are the people's placenta,
a uterus to utilise us with
the nutrients
to redesign and refine
our nature that nurtures
the stone from which our blood is drawn.

The Ouroboros

'What the hell is this?
Do *you* know what it is?
I don't know what it is!
I'm chucking it!'

My father,
is a cartoon mole
burrowing into cupboards
cascading unwanteds across the room.

Black bags of the patched-up and tattered,
the sewed-up, re-stitched and torn.
A stitch in time saves nine
but they've had ten,
so it's time to go.

Like the Olympics,
the same rigmarole every four years.
a different site built,
even bigger than the last
before being left to stand,
an unused reminder
to the next host,

a scar of a time
unwilling to leave.

This year, the front room hosts
the opening ceremony of rhetorical questions;
'Do you use this?
Do you need it?
Did you even know it was there?
There's three of the buggers here—!'

A hoarded fungus
in uncategorised mounds.
'It's shapeshifting!
The same bloody things, just in a different place.
Up to your neck in junk!
You've got to chuck it out.'

Socks, scarves, Sunday supplements,
bills, letters, notes —
  'Fetch catalogues & magazines from next door – Mam'
  'Gone up the tip – Dad'
  'Fetch milk, bleach, papers, and bread – Mam'
  'Taken stuff to the tip – Dad'

'Things creep in without you realising,
and before you know it,
the stuff's everywhere!
You've got to check this house regular
or you don't know what you'll find.'

The Ouroboros – The snake that devours itself.
'It's never ending.
This crap never seems to leave.'

Attempting to start small,
one piece at a time.
'We're going to have to do it together.
I'll do this section, you start over there...'
merely opens a space
to be refilled.

*

A mole.
'If it's over 1.6mm, it could spread...'
Things creep in without you realising.
'But it's so small. Can't they just cut it out?'
Before you know it, you can't even move.

If you don't check regular
you don't know what you'll find.
'It's the same thing, just in a different place.'

'What the hell is this?'
'Do *you* know what it is?'
'I don't know what it is!'
'Chuck it!'

Chuck it, then Dad
Chuck it out
Chuck it out Dad
Just chuck it
Chuck it out
Chuck it out, Dad
Dad, chuck it out
Chuck it out
Chuck it out
Chuck it out

Chuck it out...

70

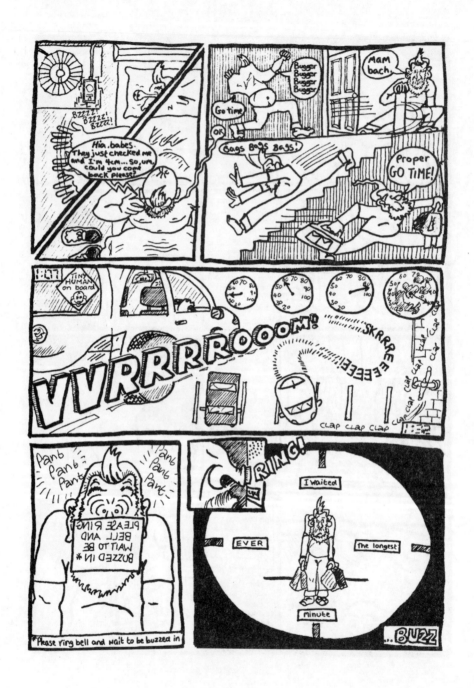

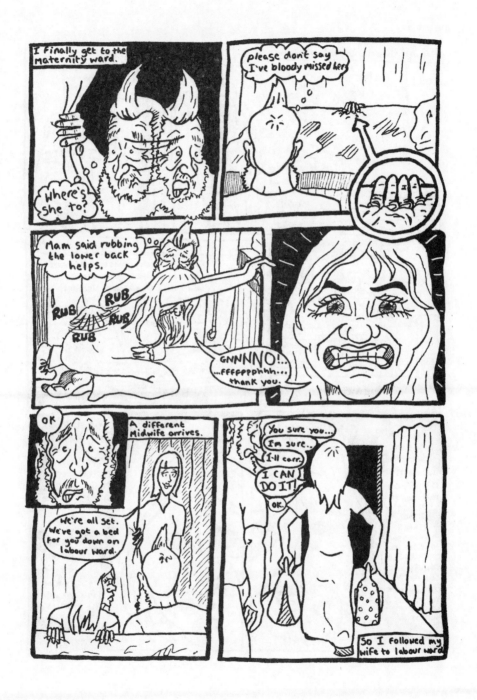

74

76

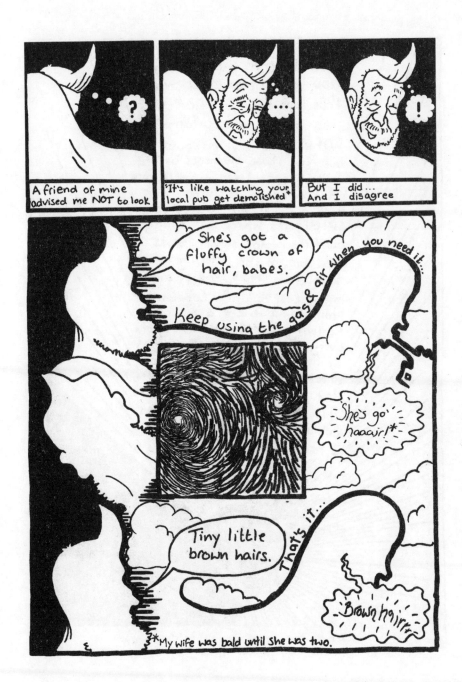

A new father once told me
"You have never experienced
true love until your first child
is put into your arms"
Of which I had no doubt,
but in those moments before,
I had never loved my wife more.
We had known eachother for
half our lifetime. Highschool
sweethearts who'd met during
our first major school tests
and through the following years
had seen every major and
minor test of life together.
From living in the same town
to living apart for three years.
Every job, every anxiety, every
smile, every tear, every first.
First kiss, first dance, first house,
first dance as husband and wife.
This woman, who's hand I was
holding throughout another first,
I loved more than anything
in this world

And then my daughter was born.

The
Beginning...

The Butterflies of Anxiety

Gasps, quickening.
I shake,
clenched jaw,
to hide the spasms
distorting me.
Trying to escape
tendons almost rupturing,
contorting me.
Stomach, churning, empty
like the cavity of a burnt-out car.

'Please don't die.'

Slipping out into the rain
you find that spark
in the ignition,
to start again
over that dreadful mountain.
The road, a twisted grimace, gleaming.

You are a wonderful driver.
He is not.

At the top,
passing over the grid, on the bend,
you cross paths.
A dangerous dance,
gliding towards you,
fingertips smashing,
holding you tightly before the tilt.
bending and swaying
to the beat of pounding hearts.

Shattered blown-dandelion stems of glass,
– wisps of life –
lifting above the barrier,
leaving a blasted shell of black metal,
no longer hard, but dough
being rolled and rolled and rolled
down that dreadful mountain.

Bouncing.

Like a baby on a father's knee,
until crashing to a deafening stop.
A chrysalis of mourning
from which nothing will emerge.

Yet you're still by my side,
comforting me.

'Please don't die,' I whisper.

Just Like His Father

KICK OFF

'Gambo's a big fucka, butt,' said Mevin (fly half).

Gwilym 'Gambo' Bowen was the first choice prop forward for Aberreba rugby football club first XV. As strong as an ox and looked like one too, if you tattooed 'Muriel' on its shoulder and two eyes on its arse.

'They say a good big fucka will always beat a good little fucka,' said Idwal (flanker), calling a spade a shovel but still getting his point across.

'Woh yew sayin' 'en?' said Bans (prop), knowing the answer.

'I'm sayin' eesa big fucka,' said Idwal, raising his hand then pointing at Bans, 'an yewra little fucka compared to 'im, no matter who's lookin atiw.' Idwal had an old-fashioned name that no one made fun of because he was hard as nails and right about most things.

Bans was pissed off at the jibe but couldn't raise a response as he'd stood next to Gambo every Tuesday and Thursday night for three years since he came up from the youth team. Four inches taller and a good three stone heavier than him, Gambo *was* a big fucka.

'E cahn geh no bigger, mind, though cun e, Id?' said Mousey (scrum-half), speeding through the sentence. 'Twinny-three now, see. Stopped growin' now, avn e. Less e's a late blooma. You a late blooma Bans? Got all yew pubes yet?' The last words tripped over Mousey's nervous laughter as he slugged his pint.

'Course e av,' yelled Mugga (centre). 'But e shaved 'em off cause they itched like fuck after e caught 'em crabs off tha' looka on oldays last Augus'.'

Jeers and laughter from the surrounding tables in the Player's Lounge.

'Dur, dirty bitch she musa bin to take a pop at yewr floppy three-and-half, butt. Dew keeper knickers?' Mugga sniffed his fingers before rubbing them under Bans nose.

'Fuck off!' Bans pushed his hand away. 'Serious this is by'uh, mun! I'm stuck in no man's land!'

Four weary heads, a table away, turned towards him like water buffalo disturbed mid-graze.

'Watch y'mouth now Bansy, boy,' Mal said cooly. 'There's fourteen other men y'uh happy enough to show you th'way to subsville if y'carry on.'

Mal, forty-three, along with Bill Dare and Dai Tapp, both forty, and Graham Lout, forty-one, (all forwards) stared silently at Bans. The Old Guard, emphasis on the 'ard. Nobody plays rugby past forty unless you're stupid or solid and these boys weren't stupid.

Ken (lock forward), unscrewed the jar of pickled onions, picked one out and leaned over to Bans, 'If you don't want to vegetate. Pollinate.'

Bans scrunched up his face in typical confusion at Ken's metaphors, 'Fuxa' mean?'

Idwal tapped him on the shoulder, 'It means do sumin' 'bout it.'

'If God gives iw lemons, squeeze 'em in the fucka's eyes and pinch 'is lemonade.' Ken clarified.

'Whatever you do won't make a difference, mun,' Mousey continued. 'Gambo's only twenty-three. He've got ages left in him.'

'Cheers butt. Fuckin' lovely that is. Really.' Bans tried to flick a beermat at Mousey but it clung to the table. 'Fuxake.'

'Sayin' I am, that's all. Builder inee? Lumpin' stuff round all day's all e does, mun. Keeps iw fit 'n' strong tha' does, dwnit? I mean even when e's no' tryin', e's trainin'.'

Bans sank further down into his seat.

'Don't worry butt, I 'erd the girls say e got a tiny knob if thas any consolation,' Idwal said.

'Lies that is,' said Mugga. 'Sorry, butt. Avniw seen 'im in the showers?' He stood and swung his arm between his legs. 'Like a baby elephant's nose it is.'

'Bollocks, mun!' said Bans, rising in a huff.

'They fuckin' ewj an' all!' Mugga grabbed his crotch, as the boys bellowed laughing.

Idwal raised an eyebrow, 'Hold on now. What you bin staring at his knob for, Mug?'

'Couldn't help it, mun! He turned round to fetch his towel last week and the fucking thing almost took my eye out!' As Mugga spoke, he swung his arm towards Ken who flicked the pickled onion into the air and grabbed his eye, howling in mock cock-chopped agony. The pickled eyeball flew across the table and plopped into Ban's pint, soaking his lap and dampening his spirits even further.

'Oh fuck iew lot! I'm off for a fuckin' shit!'

The boys pissed themselves laughing, throwing beermats at Bans as he stormed across the stained and scuffed clubhouse floor.

HALF TIME

Bans sat on the toilet, his trousers round his ankles, his elbows on his knees and his head in his hands. Like an angry comic-strip character, steam rose from his body. The toilet was technically outside, even though it was linked to the main function room. The off-white tiles would sweat constantly and the only light was a fizzing fluorescent strip above the sink. The wire-meshed window opened about an inch if you were lucky, before hitting the bars on the outside, but if you had to open it at all, it meant someone had baked a good enough stench in there to warm the room. Then the rancid toilet was best avoided, since the stench was such that you wouldn't even last long enough to piss, rendering the toilet out of action for Health and Safety reasons.

Bans had been trying for two years to break through into Aberreba's First XV but his position (tight-head prop) was coveted by Gambo. He knew what the boys had been saying was right but he didn't want to admit that it was so obvious. Gambo was taller, broader, heavier and generally better than him. Bans wanted to be a serious rugby player yet he knew that it would take a hell of a lot more than extra training to be able to shift Gambo from the cornerstone of the Aberreba pack. But he'd be buggered if he was ever going to play for another team. There was only one other team near enough to play for and they were too near by half. Glyngelyn. He'd have to move away, change his name and his accent if he ever considered playing for them. Sworn local derby rivals and geographical enemies at approximately three miles down the valley. Absolute bastards. Filthy, stinking thugs who couldn't play tidy rugby so they'd resort to dirty tactics, off-the-ball cheap shots and mind games. They wore illegal studs so they'd draw blood when they stamped all over you in the rucks and then there were the high tackles, the sly digs in the scrum and their habit of whacking you in the bollocks whenever they ran past you. They'd key your car on the way to a match and try to shag your missus afterwards. And they made a point of never saying thank you to Moira up the club, when she served them their sausage and chips after the game. Of course, *they* say exactly the same things about Aberreba.

It was a rivalry born from decades of bi-annual local derbies. It started famously after a particularly tough match one weekend, the miners from Aberreba, on a rare occasion, got lost underground in the Twlldu Colliery and came up the shaft on the Glyngelyn side. Since everyone is black-faced underground they ended up slagging Glyngelyn off to the very men who played for Glyngelyn rugby football club.

Such rivalries have forever been fuelled by battles on the field for nothing but bragging rights settled with blood, muck and mucus for polished mantlepiece pride: the Pen-ôl Pick. Whichever side won the derby (by any means necessary), would be able to carry the coveted bronzed pickaxe back to their clubhouse, usually aloft through the streets of their hometown like celebrated heroes home from war.

The 'by any means necessary' tactic was usually appointed to specific marksmen who, with a certain skillset, could manipulate the outcome of a game based purely on single acts of courage and in most cases, self-sacrifice. These marksmen were known down the years as 'characters'. Their courage was honoured locally by never looking them straight in the eye or sitting in 'their' seat at the club. Their self-sacrifice was recognised by a chronology of league statistics from penalties through to red cards and ultimately, lifetime bans from the game of rugby football. Although with the art of doctoring names in club contracts, a lifetime was never literal.

Framed photographs of local internationally-capped schoolboys, silky-skilled scrum-halves and side-stepping wing wizards covered Aberreba's clubhouse, but those who were truly respected did not need their faces up on the nicotine-stained walls. They were ghosts of rucks and mauls, unsung champions of the early shower, those who would only need a nod or a wink as incentive to weave their magical thread of intimidation with just a hint of good old-fashioned violence. Giants like 'Talking' Tommy Stanley who would merely have to 'have a talk' with his opposite number and said player would have left the field before half time. Haydn 'The Salmon' Solomon: as the salmon would leap and leap up rivers and waterfalls, so opposition players would leap from rucks and mauls as if they had been overcome by the spirit of the striving shoals. Or Phil 'The Dentist' Moses, who did not make a living from removing teeth but was very adept at it. Nicknames bestowed on the cult heroes of grassroots foul play.

Among these men stood the primary reason Bans was adamant he was never chosen to play for the firsts. His link to a local legend: the man with no nickname, Glyn Jenkins. Glyn Jenkins wasn't a big man but he had hands like shovels and a mind as sharp as a pickaxe. He was, literally, the special arm of Aberreba's team from 1972–84. A genius of the discretionary dark arts. He could take down a star player in the blink (or rather, the gouge) of an eye, and find a way of taking the legs off an outside-half without even leaving the scrum. Referees suspected him of at least forty-eight unconscious men, twenty-seven broken bones (not including fingers), over a hundred broken noses and four, possibly five, unexplained absences of opposition players before kick-off. But his genius lay in the fact that he was never ever caught. Throughout those twelve years with Aberebba, no one actually saw him breaking a single rule of the game.

Glyn Jenkins invented the term 'the covert clout' in 1983, the same year that Sony invented the handheld camcorder, which would prove to be the catalyst to Glyn's early exit from the game. Although every referee knew of Glyn's penalty-circumventing prevalence on Saturday afternoons, they were almost unanimous in their frustration at never catching him in the act. But one Saturday afternoon, at the Gwli, Aberebba's home ground, the Sony Betamovie BMC-100P, poking out from behind the bushes at the back of the *Kev's Fish* sponsored stand, did.

Every game Glyn Jenkins played during the 1983–84 season was recorded on tape. On a sunny afternoon in May, as the eagerly anticipated highlight of the season between Aberreba and Glyngelyn for the Pen-ôl Pick was about to kick off, the Welsh Rugby Union was handed a Betamovie video cassette. This video cassette contained a compilation of every suspicion they ever had of Glyn Jenkin's infamous tactics. His guilt was grainy but undeniable.

The home changing room received a knock on the door at 2.29 pm that Saturday afternoon and Glyn Jenkins never played another game of rugby.

He received three successive life bans for four full pages of sighting offences, not including copping off with one referee's wife as she waited outside the changing rooms. The memory still rankles Aberreba players and supporters alike, as the loss that fateful afternoon was the end of their eleven-year unbeaten run against Glyngelyn. The Pen-ôl Pick has been begrudgingly handed back and forth like the village copy of *Debbie does Dallas*, ever since.

Though rumour and inter-clubhouse committee gamesmanship accusations were levied against Glyngelyn, the film-maker remains anonymous to this day. Many suspect they may be in the WRU's witness protection programme somewhere in north Wales.

Glyn took his exit from the game badly and couldn't bring himself to return to the club-house, not even for a pint after the match. Cutting him from the game he loved was too much; the wound too deep. He returned only once, coaxed after a few beers to the summer disco where he met the woman he was to marry, Charlamaine Pugh. A few years later they had a son, Michael. Aberreba has a population of 1528, one road in and the same road out, one pub, one shop, a post office and a school. The boy, traditionally bored, as so many before him, was inevitably drawn to the social hub that was Aberreba RFC.

Nicknames are a badge of acceptance in bastions of physical and psychological dominions, and just like in the shower room, everyone is eventually compared. So they honoured a fallen soldier by initiating his offspring in the only way a small town rugby club knew how. Michael Glyn Jenkins would be passed the mantle of the eponymous 'man with no nickname' via a moniker that would have awaited his father, had he returned: Bans.

But this, to Bans' constant despair, carried the burden of association in the eyes of every official. Even though Bans could not grow a moustache anywhere near the virility of his father's and lacked the distinctive butter-wouldn't-melt blue eyes, he was still unmistakably the man with no nickname's son. Bans was constantly looked upon with questioning eyebrows raised by referees, as they checked studs before the match. They would be halfway through musing, 'I'm sure I know you from somewhere...' when the penny dropped and their attitude towards young Michael Jenkins was forever changed.

Some referees didn't know his father. They were the matches Bans relished. Walking onto the field before kick-off he'd feel like Maria at the start of *The Sound of Music* but as soon as he was recognised he wanted to cross the Alps in clothes made from curtains, to escape the sporting prejudice that would follow. Any foul play, collapsed scrum, high tackle, punch thrown, even swearing, Bans would be on the end of a long talk from the referee, which always ended in, 'You're just like your father.'

SECOND HALF

'Ow Bans, guess wha'?' yelled Mugga as Bans shuffled back from the shithouse.

'Dwn care, butt,' said Bans

'Yew fuckin will do, butt, when I telliw,' said Mugga.

'Gambo's bust his leg.' Mousey stole Mugga's line.

''Av e?' said Bans, still believing he was being taunted.

'Aye, the fuckin' fucker's fuckin' fucked, butt. Out. Full season. Op and everything, probly.'

'Fuck off! Really?' said Bans.

'Where d'e do it to?' asked Idwal.

'Thasa best part,' said Mousey. 'E done it inis worx van. N'guess aw—? John The Bastard pulled out on Bryn Hill and Gamb ad to swerve. Ended up smashin' into a lamp post by Gill Gob's house!'

John The Bastard was Glyngelyn's gangly 6'6" second-row forward. Not the brightest spark, in fact, more of a dull glow, but in the line-out was almost guaranteed to win the ball. He was like a kite with hands. John the Kite would have suited him better but nicknames are hardly ever given on attributing merits. His nickname wasn't through chastising of his mother's premarital sins, but through the incredulous dismay of the crowd watching his first derby match. Aberreba lost by a single point, scored through a last minute accidental drop-goal fluke by none other than the player formerly known as 'Lanky' John. For the first two hours after the final whistle he was John 'The Jammy Bastard', but beer breeds contempt and he soon became simply John 'The Bastard'.

'Aviw seen 'im or is 'is bollocks again, now?' Bans wanted to be sure.

'No, tellin' iw now, Gill Gobb just rung Glyngelyn's clubhouse to try to claim compo off 'em for a fucking Council lamp post, daft twat!' Mousey was too excited for simplicity. 'She told 'em John the Bastard was an even bigger bastard f'doin what his father shoulda done.' He looked around, waiting for the inevitable question.

'Whassat 'en?' Idwal finally asked.

'Fuckin' pull out innit?!' said Mousey before spluttering into high-pitched laughter.

'Unlucky f'poor ol' Gambo, mind,' said Idwal. 'But yew might be in witha shout now, Bans,'

'Glyngelyn week Saturday and John will be in that fucking side. John the car-swerving bastard, smiling that bastard smile of his,' said Mugga

'Bastard's gonna need a fuckin' bodyguard,' said Mousey, musing the possibilities of injuries.

'Personal now, innit?' said Idwal. 'Yers yew chance, Bans boy.'

But Bans wasn't listening. He was already there, scoring winning tries and scrummaging like a rhino as the crowd chanted his name.

Over the next few hours Bans drank as if they had already won the Pen-ôl Pick. The great Gambo-shaped boulder had rolled back down to the bottom of the hill and his Sisyphus-like struggle for a place in the Firsts was over.

By ten o' clock a well-oiled Bans sat in the corner of the clubhouse like the cat that got the creamflow, when Bill Dennis, the Firsts' coach, bald, twice-broken jaw with ears more cauliflower than cartilage, walked into the bar. He greeted everyone with his trademark of adding 'Big' to the start of everyone's names – Big Ken, Big Id, Big Mugga – apart from Moira and the barmaids; they were always 'love'.

After noticing Bans he made a beeline, sat down next to him and began speaking to him fervently. The boys watched as Bans initially furrowed his brow and shook his head in acknowledgment of the severity of Gambo's injury before nodding, beaming and then shaking Bill's hand like he was wagging a tail. Bill pulled an approving jib and tapped him on the back.

Without hearing what was said, they all knew Bans had finally been asked to 'step up', 'work hard' and 'man for man, pound for pound' prove his worth. His invite to the Firsts was finally here.

But now Bill moved in closer to speak to him, his eyes taking on the steely determination that had kept him coach for the last seven years. They *would* beat Glyngelyn, by any means necessary. So long as someone was willing to make the necessary sacrifices. He was giving Bans his own private pre-match speech, snarling and grinding his teeth as he spoke, passion flaring to contempt for the long-standing rivals of the club.

But Bans' high spirits appeared to ebb away as he listened. He was not engaging in the visceral battle cry of Bill Dennis. Instead his demeanour took on a slow transformation, a cold realisation that this personal triumph was not a sporting promotion but a successive legacy returning to haunt him. Bans had been tallying up a familiar record, taking the whistle blows and receiving the punishments of team mates' penalties and match-time misdemeanours. It had not gone unnoticed. He had knocked out so-and-so, stamped on whatshisname and taken the consequence on the chin. Without realising, Bans had deluded himself to believing that his call up was for a display of improvement. He had become his father's son.

Bans rose from his seat and shouted, violently shaking his head trying to deny the portrait that was being painted of him. Drunk and confused with emotion, he banged his fist on the table.

Bill pointed at Bans and then at the crest of the club above the bar and as the club quietly turned to listen, Bill looked him straight in the eye and said something slow and deliberate: '... It's not always about you, it's about the club.'

Wild-eyed, Bans took leave of his senses and picked up the jar of remaining pickled onions, veered around enraged and launched it at the crest. It shattered, cascading its contents across the room, tearing the wallpaper. Pickled onions pelted anyone unlucky enough to be near the bar and soaked the rest in vinegar. His chest heaving, he stood as the club fell silent, everyone staring at him.

He seemed to wake from the episode and was taken aback when Moira shouted from the bar, the inevitable sentence of any unwarranted violent behaviour at the clubhouse, 'Bans, you're banned!'

Bans left the clubhouse and ran home down the gwli behind the club. The sun, almost setting above Aberreba, streamed over the terraced rooftops, illuminating the drystone details of backgarden walls, zinc-roofed sheds and runner-bean-poled allotments. A mongrel terrier, mid-squat in the shadow of the chapel vestry, barked and scrambled out of Bans' path just as a size ten dap left a perfect footprint in the dog's steaming metaphor. As Bans ran, it slowly dawned on him that not only had he shamed himself and would have to wait for the committee to decide whether they would allow him back to the clubhouse, but his chances of ever playing for the Firsts were as shattered as the pickle jar.

As the boys watched his silhouette disappear down the gwli, one of the old stalwarts sipped his pint, 'He's nothing like his father.'

FINAL WHISTLE

Cawl

The leaves had fallen by this time of year and carpeted the winding lane in brown, red and yellow, the colour of rotting meat. The two men drove several miles through the woods before seeing the tip of the small chimney, smoke whispering into the trees around the cottage. The front door was glossed red like a Royal Mail pillar box. They went to knock just as it opened and Mrs Frank's statuesque figure filled the doorway, followed by the smell of her infamous cooking. She squared up inches from their faces, her eyes adjusting to the light, dissolving her pupils to darkening pools.

'Good morning, Officers!' she said with a smile, like drawing back a leather curtain on marble headstones.

'Good afternoon, Mrs Frank,' said Officer Harris. 'This is Officer McCann. He's from the city, come to assist...'

'...With the investigation, yes, yes, I know all about it,' she interrupted, turning to McCann. 'You've come all this way.'

'How have you...?' McCann began.

'What else would people be talking about, you silly man? There's been a little girl missing, for goodness sake!'

McCann was taken off guard. He was used to being called many things in the city, but he had never been scolded as a silly man by an elderly lady with a blue-rinse perm and forearms bigger than his own. This was a far call from investigating 'missing' gang members in rundown tower blocks.

'We need all the help we can get.' Mrs Frank, looked over her spectacles at Harris, who fiddled with his belt and avoided eye contact. 'So they've sent us you.'

'It's always good to have another set of eyes look over things afresh,' said McCann.

'Hmm. Well, it's a fair old drive through them woods from the station. You'll come in for something to eat?' she said, more of a command than an invite. She turned for them to follow.

'We'd like to take a look around,' said McCann. Mrs Frank paused halfway down the passage.

'Why's that then?' She asked, turning her head and narrowing her eyes.

McCann tried to gauge her reaction in the gloom of the passage. 'Well, you're the only house near to where...'

'Fine, but downstairs only, mind,' she interrupted with the wave of her hand. 'I haven't started on upstairs, yet, this morning,' she disappeared into one of the doorways. 'I'll see what I've got for you. A drop of stew, maybe.'

'That won't be necessary...'

Harris held an arm out to McCann with a slight look of panic and shook his head.

'What was that?' called Mrs Frank returning to the passage.

'We'd love to, Mrs Frank.' Harris said.

Mrs Frank grunted and then was out of sight again.

'It's easier just to eat something,' Harris whispered to McCann.

McCann raised his eyebrow at Harris, closed the door behind them and the passage suddenly plunged into darkness.

The doorway was the only source of light apart from some sunlight from a small window up the staircase and the room that Mrs Frank had disappeared into, undoubtedly the kitchen. McCann took the liberty of turning on a light switch which did little but dimly reveal a few frames hanging on the dark, wood panelled walls. Faceless people wandering through an industrial landscape, two Lowry prints looked all the more haunting and lonely in the sombre glow of a single bulb. One of Francis Bacon's grotesque portraits hung on the opposite wall. That one even looked like an original but was probably a very good fake. It was difficult to judge in the light.

Halfway down the passage, past a brass hook upon which nothing hung, was another deeper frame. McCann looked closer to see a display of trinkets. Coins, buttons, a piece of cloth with half an indistinct emblem, a black feather, a piece of string tied in a knot, a theatre ticket stub and, at the very centre, a tooth. Each item was clipped to the backboard with small twisted wire. Engraved on a small brass plaque at the bottom of the frame was a date and a dash, '1965–'. There seemed to be a few spaces yet to be filled. McCann motioned to Harris, who studied the display but shrugged his shoulders. McCann was already picking up some discrepancies from the reports he'd read about the investigation. From his brief time with Harris, his policing techniques seemed to be a little more... rural than McCann had been lead to believe.

A shadow fell over them.

'People lose all kinds of things in these woods,' said Mrs Frank.

Her silhouette reflected between the two in the glass. She was taller than them both and her features were lit by the light from the landing window, her nose was bulbously similar to the doorknob of the *cwtch* under the stairs. The only door with a key in the lock, McCann noticed.

'They always seem to belong to little boys,' she said motioning to the frame.

'A tooth?' asked McCann. 'How did you find a tooth in these woods?'

'Stuck in the side of a tree. Must've tripped and fallen into it. Boys will be boys.'

'Girls can trip and fall,' said McCann. 'And everyone has teeth.'

Mrs Frank stared at McCann in the glass; he held her gaze. Suddenly she shot her false teeth out at him. McCann recoiled from the reflection and bumped backward into her standing behind him. She caught her teeth and roared with laughter. 'Not *everyone* has teeth, Officer McCann.'

Still laughing she put her teeth back in then turned back to the kitchen, quickly removing the key from the lock behind her and dropping it into the pouch of her apron. Harris followed her while McCann hung back, embarrassed at being frightened by a toothless old woman. As he followed them he saw that the passage continued through to a back entrance with another door at the far end, which looked like it could lead to a cellar.

As McCann entered the kitchen he was struck by how bright it was compared to the passage. The large window above the Belfast sink looked out onto a herb garden at the back of the house with dense woods beyond it. Harris had already started on a plate of cheese and cold meats that was placed on the red and white gingham tablecloth. McCann stayed standing near the door. 'Do you mind if I take a look downstairs, Mrs Frank?' he asked.

'Downstairs?' she asked. McCann noted her surprise.

'There's nothing downstairs but damp and demijohns for my sloe gin. I can fetch them up for you, but they won't be ready 'till next month at least.' she said. 'C'mon, sit,' she motioned to the plate. 'To tide you over.' She lit the stove, moved a large blackened pot above the flame and stirred its contents.

'It's not so much the sloe gin I'm interested in,' McCann said.

'Like I said, the only other thing down there is damp. And some of Elwyn's rusty old tools.'

'All the same...' McCann said, and then smiled.

'At least eat something first,' she said, taking a step towards him, folding her hands in her apron's pouch. 'I don't get many visitors, and it's only me up here since Elwyn died so it'll only go to waste if you don't.'

They both stood facing each other as Harris, hunched over the plate, picked at the pieces of meat and cheese. McCann hadn't noticed how loud Harris' chewing was until he took a large bite of cheddar. The slapping of his lips echoed on the flagstone floor, keeping time with a distant ticking sound from somewhere in the house.

'I won't take no for an answer,' she insisted, taking another step closer and breathing heavily through her nose.

McCann reluctantly pulled out a heavy chair from the table and sat. 'Do you mind me asking how your husband died?'

Mrs Frank gasped dramatically and held her apron to her face, almost a pantomime of grief. She swatted the question at Harris with a sob, and turned to face the stove. Harris chewed quickly in an attempt to reply, crumbs of cheese falling down his shirt and onto the tablecloth.

'An accident, Officer McCann. Mr Frank was found in the woods...' began Harris.

'Poisoned!' shrieked Mrs Frank.

McCann raised an eyebrow at Harris.

'Uh, well... not so much... uh...' said Harris.

'Poison it was and everyone knows it. Somebody poisoned him when he was out on his walk,' she said, rummaging in a cupboard.

'He suffered a heart attack, Officer McCann, you see,' continued Harris, peeling a string of fat off some ham. 'But unfortunately there were confusing elements about his death, which caused some to speculate...'

'Confusing, my eye!' Mrs Frank wheezed as she bent to fetch something from the cupboard.

'Mr Frank was a large man and not partial to exercise,' Harris whispered over the table to McCann.

'Elwyn was as fit as a fiddle!' yelled Mrs Frank from the bowels of a corner unit. 'I fed him well and he was never wanting! But that day, off he went into the woods...' Mrs Frank's eyes peered from behind the cupboard door. 'They found him, with his clothes all torn and his eyes...' Her face twisted into a terrifying grimace, blue-veined cheeks flushing red, eyes bloodshot with strain. '...And his tongue lolling out of his head like a bloodhound.' She rose from the cupboard quickly with a large copper saucepan and brought it down hard on the worktop. 'Poisoned!'

'Why do you think anyone would want to poison your husband, Mrs Frank?' asked McCann.

'Jealousy. Of his lifestyle.' she said.

She poured water into the pan and placed it on the counter, then picked a handful of vegetables from the tray and began to peel them methodically.

'We came back here from Luton, where we were happy, because Elwyn needed to get things in order after his mother passed.' She crossed her chest and then pointed at the ceiling with a half-peeled carrot. '"Ancestral", he said it was. We made it a home. But too comfortable, he became. Me, cooking every day for him, while he did what he pleased. Drove to fetch the papers every morning, back every afternoon, to sit and read in the parlour. His mother left us money and he took up idleness. Didn't want to leave after a few months of that. Why would he?' She began to halve and quarter the carrots. 'Some get very jealous of that lifestyle.' She narrowed her eyes at McCann. 'But I bet whoever did poison him never spared a thought for me.' She scraped the carrots off the board into the pan. 'Left up here with no one to feed or care for. What's a woman to do?'

'Who do you believe would want to poison your husband?'

'The swede,' she turned around to look at McCann.

'Excuse me? Who's that?' he asked, taking out his notebook.

'What? That swede, there.' She pointed to the box of dirt-covered vegetables in a box next to the door.

McCann picked up a swede the size of a small child's head and held it up to Mrs Frank who took it from him and began to wash it in the sink. She cupped it in her hand and let the water wash over it before picking off the pieces of earth from the skin. She scoured the dirt from it then placed it on the chopping board. She picked up a small knife from the block and began to draw it along the skin until it coiled around her wrist, revealing the pale flesh beneath.

'Did you know that you can poison someone with rhubarb leaves?' asked Mrs Frank. 'Very popular vegetable, rhubarb. Very easy to grow. Anyone with a veg patch or an allotment could have poisoned him. You only need the slightest reason and the right vegetable. Next thing you know...' She drew the knife along her throat and stuck her tongue out.

The shrill oven timer sounded. Mrs Frank left the swede in the sink, opened the oven door and took out a tall square tin with a pair of oven mitts. Both men were instantly hit by the smell of fresh bread. With a long knife, she eased the loaf out onto a rack by the window to cool. She dusted the crown's crust with flour and returned to the stove. She ladled out two steaming bowls of stew into Pyrex bowls and placed them before the officers.

'Only something small,' she said. Harris smiled and immediately plunged his spoon in to the bowl. He blew gently on it before raising it to his lips, slurping louder than necessary.

McCann sighed at Harris, who ignored him. Mrs Frank stood over that table with her hands clasped. She fixed McCann with a smile, glanced at his bowl then back at him. Harris looked over at McCann and tried to get his attention by widening his eyes at the bowl before him.

'Cawl, officer McCann,' said Mrs Frank. 'Stew. Meat, veg, potatoes. You've had cawl before surely?'

McCann looked up at them both, and caught his lips beginning to curl in disgust before smiling up at Mrs Frank.

'Of course. Thank you, Mrs Frank. But like I said, this isn't necessary.'

She continued to stare at McCann, her grip tightening, creaking her joints. He begrudgingly picked up the spoon, scooped some and raised it to his lips. He feigned some appreciative sounds. 'Lovely,' he said.

This satisfied her. She turned and walked back to the sink.

'What do you know about Abigail Sibley?' asked McCann.

Mrs Frank wailed again and gripped the side of the sink. 'Poor soul! Lost and frightened in the woods! Four months she's been up there now.' She pulled open a drawer. 'She's either terrified, poor thing or...'

'Or what?'

McCann saw the sheen of a large bread knife.

'I dread to think...'

Mrs Frank took the loaf from the rack and cut a wedge of a crust. She cut two more slices and spread thick butter over them until they glistened. She took away the plate of meats and cheese that Harris had polished off and replaced it with the bread. Harris snatched the crust, tore it in half and plunged it into his bowl before McCann even looked up. He let it soak up the juices before taking a bite out of it. McCann hadn't noticed how out of shape Harris was. He could see his shirt bulging at the buttons, reminding him of a dressed ham. He seemed to be swelling before him. As Harris bit into the bread, the juices ran down his chin. McCann felt repulsed by him.

'Up here,' McCann said, turning to Mrs Frank.

'Pardon?!' asked Mrs Frank, turning back to McCann.

'The town is seven miles *down* the valley through the woods. Abigail left to come *up here*, to the woods. Why would an 11-year-old girl go wandering all that way into the woods? What else is further up than here, Mrs Frank?'

She ran her tongue along her teeth and stared at McCann. 'I live here, is why. Anywhere other than *here* is *up* there or *down* there,' she spoke lower. 'And we've looked. We've been looking in these woods for four months.'

McCann heard the ticking again, tick tick tick. Maybe a grandfather clock in one of the rooms.

'Was she coming up to see you?'

'Why would she be coming up to see me? I barely knew the girl.'

'You lead the first search, though, am I right?' continued McCann.

'Made sense that I should be the one to lead it. I'm up here anyway. Who else was going to do it? Him?!' She pointed at Harris, who paused and looked up from shovelling stew into his mouth.

McCann turned and saw that Harris was sweating as he ate. Glistening beads had formed on his temples. He had already finished most of his stew. McCann turned towards the doorway. The sound was an irregular tapping, unlike a clock, more like a radiator.

'The poor little lamb, she's still up there, now, somewhere. Lost and scared. And you're just sitting here asking silly questions while your food goes cold.'

'We're beginning to think she may not be... lost.'

Mrs Frank spun around suddenly with the knife in her hand, 'So you're saying that you think something has happened to her?'

McCann sprung from his seat, his reflexes used to knives being brandished at him, but not by old widows in aprons. Harris paused mid-mouthful as Mrs Frank looked at McCann strangely before focusing on the knife in her hand.

'What on earth's the matter now, Officer McCann?' She smiled coyly at him and calmly returned the knife to the counter. 'More bread?'

McCann sat back down as Mrs Frank placed some more heavily buttered bread onto the plate, which Harris duly tore to wipe up the last of his stew.

The tapping persisted. Tap tap taptap tap.

'Did Abigail ever visit you?' asked McCann.

'I've told you, not many do,' she turned to look out at the herb garden with the dirt road beyond it. 'People pass but not many that I know. Walkers mainly, now, since they showed it on that television programme.'

A famous weatherman made a brief intro to the labyrinth of forestry walks by walking past Mrs Frank's house during one episode of a popular nature show.

'They like to look at the house but they never come in... What do they think I'm going to do, eh?'

'Some people find it intriguing, maybe a little unsettling, seeing a house all the way up here in the woods. It's usually the type of thing you see or hear about in stories,' said McCann.

'What stories?' Mrs Frank asked.

'Children's fairytales,' said McCann. 'Hansel and Gretel, Little Red Riding Hood. The little old lady that lives in the woods.'

'What are you trying to say?' Mrs Frank raised her voice. 'Am I to be the wicked witch that lives to frighten children?! Hansel and Gretel were eaten, weren't they?'

McCann, picked at the slice of bread in the middle of the table. 'Breadcrumbs,' he said. 'They were saved by breadcrumbs that guided her home.'

'Them,' she said, staring at McCann. 'There were two of them, to help each other out.'

McCann could hear the tapping again, louder this time. Taptap tap. 'Sorry, what's making that noise?'

'What noise?' Mrs Frank tilted her head to listen. Harris did the same.

The tapping grew louder. Tap, taptap, tap, tap, TAP.

'That.' McCann said, emphasising with his finger.

'Radiators,' piped Harris, his mouth full of bread.

'I don't have central heating, Lewis,' dismissed Mrs Frank. 'No, that's just the house. There's not much silence in a house this old. Always something making noises. Creaking, groaning, tapping. At night, between the trees, the animals and these walls, the racket they make, you'd swear the dead were rising up.' She crossed her chest again then banged on the passage wall.

The tapping stopped.

'There are worse things to be frightened of than four walls and the wind, Officer McCann.'

'There most definitely are,' McCann replied, locking eyes with her. The silence between them thickening like gravy.

The radio exploded into sound. 'Yn y Boreeeeeee. Yn y Boreeeeeee...' A song filled the kitchen in a language McCann didn't understand. Mrs Frank's heaving bosom swelled as she screeched in an absurd falsetto to finish the chorus. She drew her hand across the room as she held the final note. McCann's grip tightened on the arm of the chair as Harris erupted in applause like a seal. Mrs Frank graciously hushed him with a pantomime dame smile.

'Just like that Community Hall concert again, Mrs Frank,' Harris beamed. Mrs Frank mock blushed.

'Oh, don't be so soft, that was a million years ago,' she returned to the oven, switching off the radio alarm as she passed. 'Before I lost my soul...' she trailed off.

'Mrs Frank?' asked McCann.

'I stopped singing after Elwyn died,' she proclaimed. 'The music in my soul died along with him.'

'Hmm.' McCann raised an eyebrow.

'Is that a pie?' Harris said, spotting the cloth draped over a plate near the window.

'Mincemeat and onion,' said Mrs Frank, smiling at Harris. 'Still hungry, Lewis?' Here you are...' She cut a quarter of it, placed it before him and took away his bowl. She paused at McCann's.

'Officer McCann, something wrong with my cooking? You haven't touched your stew.'

Harris looked up in shock as if he hadn't noticed. 'No, it's very nice... I'm just not very hungry.'

'Would you rather pie?' She placed it on the table before he could contest.

'No thank you.'

Mrs Frank began to look agitated.

McCann continued with his questioning. 'We've heard that you spoke to Abigail before she went missing. You were seen speaking to her in the town outside the hair salon.'

'She's a skinny little girl,' said Mrs Frank through her teeth. 'Not right for a girl her age to be so small. I was concerned that she wasn't being fed properly,' she said. 'Her father's a doctor, for goodness sake. He should know.'

'Why were you in town that day?'

'My hair, if we were talking outside the salon, obviously.'

Harris coughed loudly, gasped and spluttered some pie onto his plate. McCann shot him a look. Harris held a hand to his throat and tried to catch his breath.

The tapping began again, even louder. Tap tap TAP TAP.

'Piece of gristle?' asked Mrs Frank.

Harris shook his head and held his hand up in apology as he began to breathe regularly again. 'S'fine, now, Mrs Frank. Down the wrong hole.'

McCann frowned at Harris, then turned his attention back to Mrs Frank who had taken the swede from the sink and placed it on the chopping board. 'Was she upset when you spoke to her?'

'Her? No. I was. Worried sick at the state of her. All skin and bone.'

She took out a large cleaver from the drawer and flicked the underside of her nail against the blade to check it. Tap TAP TAP.

'She was fine when I spoke to her. But I told her if she kept on the way she was there'd be nothing left of her.'

She raised the cleaver and aimed for the heart of the swede. TAP TAPTAPTAP.

'All this dieting lark that young girls do, shouldn't be allowed.'

She swung the cleaver down.

'Ahhhhhhh!!' she screeched and clutched her hand. Blood began to rise up through her fingers, colouring her knuckles and dripping red onto the chopping board. A pool began to form around the halved vegetable.

'Mrs Frank!' McCann rose from his chair and grabbing her injured hand, tried to guide her to the sink. She swung it away from him, throwing droplets across the window and porcelain sink.

'Harris, for Chri'sake! Stop stuffing your face and get the car!'

Harris stumbled to his feet as if he was unaware of what had just happened. His stomach looked as if it had doubled in size and shook as he stood. 'Where are we going?'

'To the hospital, of course,' McCann said.

'Hospital?' asked Harris.

'There is no bloody hospital!' scoffed Mrs Frank, running her hand under the tap. 'Where the hell do you think you are? The nearest hospital is thirty miles away.'

'You need to sort that hand, Mrs Frank,' said McCann.

'Up here, we make do, Officer McCann.' She held up her other hand to show a series of small scars. He turned to Harris who held up his own hands to reveal a cluster of small white marks on right hand and a longer scar near his left wrist.

'You need to be self-sufficient to live here.' She smiled at McCann. 'Lewis, fetch the first aid box and the glue, you know where it is.'

Harris left the kitchen. McCann heard the front door go.

'Where do you keep your first aid box, Mrs Frank?' he asked.

'In the car. Could you please fetch me a clean towel from the hook in the passage, Officer McCann?' she asked.

McCann could see Harris through the window huffing up through the herb garden, towards the shed near the dirt road.

'Where's your car ke...'

'Officer McCann, the towel, please! I'm bleeding all over the kitchen and I've just mopped in here!'

McCann left the kitchen to walk down the passage. He squinted in the gloom to find the hook. As he passed the *cwtch* under the stairs, he saw a smaller set of hooks with three dishcloths hanging on each. He bent down to fetch one. Something caught his eye. A child's face smiling at him. He opened it out and saw twenty seven hand drawn little faces with dotted eyes and crooked smiles. Below a faded red stain was '*Ysgol Gynradd Coed-y-Forwyn 1986*'.

Taptap.

He moved his thumb over the school class towel to reveal a smaller drawing of a girl with pigtails and a smile that seemed to split her face in half.

Taptaptap.

Beneath it, a tiny scrawl.

The tapping was undoubtedly coming from the *cwtch* under the stairs.

Abigail.

McCann looked back at the kitchen doorway. He tapped back gently on the door. Tap. Tap.

He immediately heard something brush along the floor behind the door. McCann unclenched his fist and held up the key he had slipped out of Mrs Frank's pocket before he put her hand under the tap. He inserted the key and turned the lock as the front door was thrown open, flooding the passage with light for a few moments before Harris' bulk cast a shadow along the floor.

McCann shielded his eyes from the glare and adjusted his gaze to the *cwtch*.

Something was there. He could hear something shuffling along the floor.

Harris was out of breath. His nose whistled like a kettle. He came to stand next to McCann, his breath stank of mincemeat.

As Harris moved, the light slowly revealed a dirty yellow dress and a small chubby wrist. Then a face, blackened with dirt and matted hair, eyes sunken and dark, but cheeks bloated and red, lips covered in a dried brown coating. Her stomach bulged out as she sat against the wall, like a folded sack of flour. He looked down and saw that one of the girl's legs wasn't under her dress.

McCann could feel the heat radiating off Harris' bulk. He pulsed like a simmering casserole bubble set to burst. McCann crouched down and was hit by a mix of Harris body odour and the nest of filth behind the *cwtch* door.

The girl moved towards them suddenly and revealed a soaked and bloodied rag tied around a stump of a knee. She made a gargling sound from her dirt covered mouth. She no longer had a tongue. She opened her mouth as if expecting to be fed like a toddler revealing a gap in her two front teeth.

The colour drained from McCann's face. The girl reached out a hand towards the officers with only two surviving fingers.

Harris heaved before vomiting at their feet.

The girl's eyes widened. Instead of recoiling from Harris' retching, she pounced on the pool of stew and mincemeat and began to scoop it towards her, cupping as much as she could, making low sounds as she wolfed it into her mouth and licking everything from her hands. She used her two hooked fingers to scratch a piece of carrot from between the floorboards and pushed it into her mouth through the gap in her teeth. Her guttural enthusiasm dribbled down her chin, falling onto her threadbare cardigan. Scraping her hands across the floor, she paused when she felt something hard. She picked out a small object.

A ring.

She stared at the ring and cocked her head. Sunlight suddenly reflecting off the frame of trinkets in the passage, revealed the tip of a gemstone. It shone, reflected in her darkened eyes, like the last hope in the world. She smiled and slid it on one of her remaining fingers.

'You're cleaning that up yourself, Lewis,' came a voice from the passage.

McCann stumbled and fell backwards against the *cwtch* door.

'Sorry, Mrs Frank, but I'm not used to all this running after a feed,' said Harris as McCann frantically tried to reach for his radio.

'Couldn't you have used the cleaver like last time instead of making me fetch the hatchet all the way up the shed?'

'Not with this one, Lewis,' said Mrs Frank. 'Mind your eyes, now then, and hold down his arms, like we practised...'

God Bless 'Merica

The guy next door was always working on his house. He was usually sweating in the heat, his forehead shining, and his thick black beard must have made him even hotter. He'd tie his hair up by wrapping something around his head. He always did this. No matter how hot it was. His hand-drawn plans would be laid out in his dusty yard, held down by large stones on each corner. He had a small blanket under the olive tree where he'd take a break just after midday. He kept a jug of water and a bowl next to the rug. He never drank it, even though it was probably thirsty work; he only ever washed with it.

He'd been building an extension at the back of his house for years. It was a porch with a frame that would house his son's room above it, but he insisted on these fancy pillars instead of your standard four-corner structure. 'Five pillars for my children' he called them. He insisted that the foundations of these pillars would be the most important part. People would sit on the porch and if these pillars weren't stable then the whole tower would come crashing down on top of them.

I'd seen his son in the window a couple of times but never outside. He was like the character in that book at school who always stays indoors and looks out of the window then comes out and attacks someone or saves a girl or something, I can't remember. I wave at him, sometimes he waves back.

My dad would say that it was nice to see someone else who worked hard on something important like he did. I never understood how he saw it as 'important work'. I didn't see how it was any different to building model ships or gardening. The difference between my dad and the guy next door though, is I could sit and watch the guy next door working. I wasn't allowed anywhere near my dad's since it was locked in a specially-sealed room in the basement. My dad told me to never ever go near it, especially when he wasn't there, but he was always down there anyway. It's kind of like a photographer's dark room only it's got its own light source there that runs off a separate back-up generator to the house. But my dad doesn't photograph things, he creates them. A whole world of things. Like Dungeons & Dragons only less geeky. You'd think he'd be working for a big production company in Hollywood or something but it's just him and when he finishes he says it's gonna be The Greatest Story Ever Told.

He says it's his life's work. I know it's some kind of huge design project because of the work in the study. I'm allowed in the study, so I get to see the plans, but I don't really understand them. My dad says I'll understand them soon, but he needs to finish the manual. Uncle Moe comes every week and he dictates the manual to him, 'cause I don't think Dad's too good with words. He doesn't say much. He's more of an ideas guy. Uncle Moe brings his tablet and types it up. When it's done, Dad's gonna give it to... the patent office or something, I don't know.

Some of his drawings are crazy, man! My dad's got one hell of an imagination, I'll give him that much. They're pretty freaking scary if they're built to scale. No wonder he doesn't want me to go down there. I'd probably have nightmares for a month. But to me they're just drawings. Like I said, I don't get to see the real thing. He says that they change all the time anyways. He says that by the time I'm old enough to be trusted, he'll probably have redesigned them into something new anyway. He's always editing and updating the designs, making them smaller or bigger, adding legs or wings, smaller noses, bigger tails etc. They're real detailed designs so I guess you've got to be pretty intelligent to understand them. But, 'I'll tell you when you're older' is all I ever get.

I think he threw himself into work because of my mom. It's complicated. I live with my dad because she's with another guy. There's no bad feeling or anything, dad doesn't hate the guy she's with or anything. He works with his hands too, except he works with wood in a joinery. They just never really speak to each other. Dad only speaks to her through a mediator from Gabrielle Associates. He meets with Dad every few weeks. He makes me call him Mr G but he only ever really speaks to Dad.

My mom's pretty young so I don't think he likes to draw attention to it. It's legal and everything. It must be 'cause Dad's a stand-up guy. He always says she's the one, so he must care about her... she is pretty young. I think I kinda know how it happened, though. My dad must have gone to some sperm bank or something when he was a student, 'cause he needed the money, and my mom and her guy couldn't, y'know... so that's how Dad ended up... I got no proof or anything, that's just my theory. Theories aren't always right, though. I haven't really met her, which I know sounds weird. Living with a single dad who knows your mother but you can't see her or speak to her. He's not stopping me or anything, he just says I need to know some things first before I can move in with her, but I don't know when it'll happen. Things have to be sorted out first. I think the main reason it's taking so long is the paperwork. He always insists Mr G 'sticks to the script,' so that Mom'll understand everything that's going to happen.

I don't feel too bad about it because the way my dad talks about it, it'll be pretty exciting. He said it'll be like a fresh slate. A do-over for me, somewhere new. Like respawning in *Call of Duty*. I don't really understand how it works but if it's anything like the other stuff Dad talks about, it is probably pretty out there. He's contacted some guys from out of town to organise a barn party when I get there. I'm hoping it'll be like those crazy wild ones they have in college. Although he warned me that some of those guys can be animals. He said it'll be a party everyone will remember but at the time we got to keep it quiet, so I think he's organising a silent disco. I worked out that he's booked my favourite singers to perform, Bad Ceaser & Amy D 'cause I saw he'd written BC/AD on his calendar in December (which is great cause literally *nothing* happens in December).

I'm gonna freak when they come out but I'm gonna act all cool when it happens. I get presents too, which'll be a nice change since Dad doesn't believe in celebrating birthdays. But he said all that'll change.

I get kind of lonely 'cause my dad works six days a week and I don't really have any friends so when I finally met the kid next door who said he didn't have many either, it was pretty sweet to have something in common with someone. I was outside practicing my magic tricks. My dad makes me practice every day. He gets me books on sleight of hand, positive manipulation and some on hypnosis, but I mainly watch my *Dynamo* DVD on repeat. I watch David Copperfield too, but only 'cause I like his style.

When I was in the yard, I felt like someone was watching me; it's usually Dad, he's always watching, but this time it felt different. I looked around and the kid was actually out of the house. I waved and he waved back, so I called him over. He was dressed like his dad and probably around my age, except he'd hit puberty early and had funny little black fluff all around his face. But I couldn't really say anything, since I was rocking some lip fuzz myself and I'd tied my hair up in a top knot.

I spoke with him for a while. He was a little cagey at first and didn't really say much but when he started to loosen up, we had quite a bit in common. He told me he'd never met his mother either and he was going to be sent away soon to learn the language of his ancestors. He said his dad told him he'd need to learn his 'native tongue'. Neither of us knew any other bilingual kids in the neighbourhood, since we only ever really spoke to our dads. I told him mine could speak hundreds of languages but I'd only ever heard him speak one. He said his had told him there was only one true language and that's why he had to learn it. He didn't say what the one true language was but I suppose it wasn't American.

We spent the afternoon sat in the sun, shooting the breeze, looking at the clouds, picking out ones that looked like animals. We found fish, snakes, camels and followed tiny planes across the sky with our fingers. He said he could see a rabbit with a horn like a unicorn and a giant bird that looked like it was dropping bricks. I said I saw one of dad's designs, the big one with the huge teeth and tiny arms. The kid had no idea what I was talking about. He said he could see a crocodile walking on its hind legs. I said it was pretty similar. I got my sketchpad out and drew it for him but by the time we looked back up, the cloud had changed again.

I asked if he wanted to draw something and gave him the pad. He took it and drew some pretty patterns.

'That's cool. What's it supposed to be?' I asked.

'That's my language,' he said. 'That's how we write it.'

'What does it say?'

'They are friends one to another.'

'That's nice,' I said, which made him smile properly for the first time. It completely changed his face. His eyes shone and he looked happy.

'Hold that smile,' I said. 'I'm gonna draw you.'

'I don't know...' he said.

'Why not? Haven't you ever been drawn before?'

'There are some framed ones in the house from when I was younger. But I don't remember ever sitting for them...' he said.

'Well, what if I do you and you do me so then we can swap?'

He chewed over the idea before finally nodding, but by then his face had gone back to being serious. So I told him a story to try to make him smile again.

I told him about the time my dad threw a party before they moved in next door. Dad's not much of a party guy but this party, he invited everyone he knew. I saw more people at our house than ever before. It was bright and full, bursting with laughing and joking and singing. Everyone came dressed as all kinds of incredible birds and I got to stay up late to see their costumes. They were amazing! I could have sworn that they were real wings.

I'd never seen women at our house but there were more women at the party than I thought my dad even knew. They were the most beautiful women I had ever seen. The guys in the costumes were going nuts over them. I saw a few of them sneak out with one or two. Dad wasn't too happy when he found out that this was happening. I think he thought that since it was his party he could have first dibs or something. I was sent to bed 'cause it was late but I hid at the top of the stairs to watch. I could tell Dad was angry 'cause I could see his hand in his pocket and his forearm tensing while he was walking through the house. He keeps this thing in his pocket to squeeze to try to calm himself down. He calls it his wrath.

He was looking for this guy, Lou, who was strutting through the place like it was *his* party. Pouring drinks and telling people to make themselves at home and have a good time. When Dad finally found him, he went mad and threw his wrath at him and told everyone to get out and that the party was over.

By this time everyone was drunk and having such a good time that they didn't want to leave, but some of them were so far gone that when my dad was trying to get them to leave they were falling everywhere. I moved to the window and saw them from above. The front yard was littered with some who were so out of their heads that they were writhing around at funny angles, legs and arms intertwined like strange winged creatures, dying slowly on the ground. Others wouldn't leave so Dad started hosing them down to try to sober them up. He kept shouting that water cleanses and they should look back at what they'd done and be ashamed of themselves.

After everyone had gone, the tap wouldn't close so he just stared at the water trickling out of the end of the hose until he was standing in this huge pool in his white bathrobe. It bled out until it began to engulf those who were lying face down in the grass. At first it looked like everyone had drowned and Dad was just staring at them, but he was right, it woke them and then they got up and left. After everyone had gone, he finally got it to turn off and then started picking up the shoes two-by-two and dropping them into the big square box he kept at the back of the house. I could still hear the others talking loudly in the street around the front of the house so I went to see what they were doing. All their white costumes were ruined but they didn't seem to care, they were too busy kissing and groping each other. Then this Lou guy says that if they wanted to carry on partying they could go to his basement apartment downtown. So they all started to follow him, their wings falling off as they staggered down to the dark end of the street, their feathers blowing off into the sky.

The kid must not have liked the story as much as I did cause he didn't smile long enough for me to draw him well so I did him as a cartoon instead. The one part he did seem interested in, though, was the women. He kept asking about them and what they looked like. I described their fantastic wings and their long blonde hair and that I was sure you could see their nipples when Dad hosed them down. So I drew his cartoon with a thought bubble above his head full of women.

He looked shocked when I showed him. Then he asked if I could put more women in the bubble.

'I'll put as many as you like in,' I said, a little surprised.

'72?' he asked, his eyes wide in anticipation.

I laughed out loud.

'That's specific!' I said and we both started laughing.

We were both rolling around on the grass when his dad walked over to us and asked us what we were laughing about.

His son shot up immediately and stared at the floor. 'Nothing, we were just... talking...'

'What's that?' My neighbour pointed at the sketchpad by my feet.

'It's just my sketchpad, sir,' I said, trying to stand, clutching it to hide the drawings of the women.

'Let me see that,' he motioned for me to hand it over.

I hesitated but then gave him the pad.

He got all red in the face. 'Who is this?!' he yelled, jabbing his finger at the cartoon.

'It's just a drawing, sir.' I said. 'I drew it of your son.'

'Who do you think you are, drawing anyone you please?!' he shouted.

'I said he could keep it.' I turned to him. He stayed silent as he looked at me then back at his dad.

'I said you shouldn't do it...'

'Oh, c'mon! It's just a cartoon! People have been drawing each other for years. What's the big deal?' I asked.

'Don't you ever do this type of thing again, do you hear me?!' his dad shouted.

Our back door swung open and my dad came out and strode towards us. 'What's going on here?'

I didn't think he was home but I was glad he came out.

'Your son has been drawing my son.'

'Hey, it's nice to see you out of your room,' my dad said to the kid. 'Let me see that, son.'

I handed him my sketchpad and he started to flick through it. A smile spread across his face. He ruffled my hair and winked at me.

'Haha. He must be taking after me,' he said. 'These are good, son.'

I couldn't help but smile, even under the circumstances. He never usually praised anyone but himself.

'He's disrespecting my son by depicting him as a cartoon!' The man next door said. He must have been quite old-fashioned and thought that cartoons were like the ones you get in newspapers where they make fun of politicians. You've got to be real smart to understand them. What I'd drawn was basically a doodle with a headscarf and a thought bubble.

'No I'm not. We were laughing about it. You saw us...!'

'You need to make sure that he doesn't keep offending us like this.' He spoke directly at Dad. I didn't understand what he meant by 'keep offending them' 'cause this was the first time I'd ever even spoken to the kid outside little waves to the window.

'He's just expressing himself,' my dad said. The way they both spoke to each other now was different, as if they were carrying on a conversation they'd been having for years. 'I had my son, you had yours, that was the deal like I told you before...' He trailed off.

'Excuse me?' said Dad, glancing at me quickly. 'Don't finish that sentence.' It was like they were't talking about us anymore.

'I told you when we started this that we had very different opinions about how we wanted our sons to be brought up, Godfrey,' he said, hushed.

'Allan, you wanted to go out on your own and start your own thing. I understood and I was fine with that, but like I told you, I made my decision. You want to make your own stories with it, good luck to you – but keep your ideas and opinions out of my backyard.' They definitely weren't talking about us anymore.

'This isn't your yard,' he growled back. 'This land was ours before we separated. Not yours and mine. We agreed to share the land. That's the only thing we could agree on!'

'Well, I've changed my mind,' said my dad, narrowing his eyes, his forearm tightening in his pocket.

The kid next door looked over, expecting me to know what they were talking about, but I had no idea. They seemed far more familiar with each other than they had ever let on. The kid and I stared at each other nervously before turning back to our fathers. We both knew something was happening that would be an inevitable change in our lives.

They glared at each other for what seemed like a thousand, two thousand years.

Then my dad turned to me and said, 'Jesus, get your stuff. You're moving to your mother's.'

'America is the greatest nation on earth because of our history as a God-fearing nation. We were created as a Christian nation, and as such, we have adapted the teachings of both God and Jesus. In that way, Jesus IS American' – Christ_is_Lord – Jan 12 2013 – Topix.com

Facebook Ranting Poem

Dear RCT Council, I still don't get

This business of £75,000,000 deficit.

Cuts from Westminster, for years we've feared

But then a £75,000,000 WAG investment appeared?

So £75,000,000 for £75,000,000.

No education cuts necessary then? Brilliant!

Hold on now, 11 primary schools will still shut?

But won't that £75 mill fill the £75 cuts..?

Now I know one's investment & the other is cost

But with the data ur chuckin' about, I'm still lost.

That like for like amount's a coincidence?

Well the fact we can't use it's an inconvenience.

Then there won't b job losses, displacement or fuss

Worrying 'bout sending 3-year-olds on a school buss

With 19-year-olds from another valley,

Have you been on a school buss to Tonypandy?

So Ferndale's buggered, & Pandy & Porth,

Basically all communities first areas with their own 6th forms

Have to choose between the two T's & ten miles:

Schools of 'Excellence' at Treorchy or Tonyrefail.

One at the top & one at the bottom

& as usual the Rhondda fach is forgotten.

Outstandin', Top notch, tidy darts, crackin',

If you're 16+ from Maerdy you're sendin 'em packin'.

You're banking on theory, pandering to stats,

The sinking ship's being scrapped by the very same rats

That chewed through the rafters, & gnawed through the ropes

While complaining they don't know how they will cope

Having to steer the county through such difficult tides

Yet it's always the Leader who eventually decides

Which direction we should sail in

& who goes down with the ship when all else is failing.

So here's this poet's recommendation:

Instead of 'holding consultations'

Ask REAL people in REAL situations.

People who commute from bus stops, train stations,

Those running low on faith & on patience.

Who walk home in hail, rain, sleet & snow

With no friends in high places, just ones who know

Penury, poverty & practicality,

Hand to mouth, buy as you view, food banks & charities.

We're already 2 grand below the national annual wage,

Life expectancy 5 years less than the average age,

The 3rd largest county per geographic population

Number 1 per person in council frustration,

Yet complaints aren't reflected in local elections,

Each year votes for political stagnation.

Merge our health boards, join in with Merthyr.

Make those ambulances travel a bit further.

Let the black bags pile up & the food bins fester.

Leave the temporary remain from what once was 'a tester'.

Grow the holes in the roads, the pavements wear thin,

Why not fill them with water & charge for 'twilight swims'?

That'd solve the problem of closing the pools

& all the youth centres not attached to a school

& libraries, museums, art centres, parks,

You've already turned off the streetlamps, Our future looks dark.

Einstein – 'Insanity is doing the same every day

While looking for different results & for change'

We keep thinking that things will Improve by insistence.

We're turkeys hoping bullets will run out by Christmas.

I know how easy it is to blame

The government, parties, the council, the same.

But the thing is WE'VE done nothing wrong here

& we're paying for errors year after year.

It doesn't make sense & it isn't fair.

If your seat is broken, You'd get a new chair.

But this system is broken, it has to go

Or we'll all remain broke & collapsed on the floor,

by shifting on us what we're paying you for.

So heed this poem at County Hall,

We put up with enough shit without this nonsense and all.

131

How to Project the Country next to England:
A Recourse of Screenplays for Recognition.

Abroad – Turkey

'Where are you from?'

'Wales.'

'...?'

'In the UK.'

'England?'

'No, the country next to it.'

'Ireland?'

'Before that...'

'Near Scotland?'

'No, England, Scotland, Ireland and the other one is Wales.'

'...Oh.'

Abroad – Gran Canaria

'Where are you from?'

'Wales.'

'Walis?'

'In the UK.'

'Oh, England!'

'No, west of England.'

'Near London?'

'300 miles west of London.'

'So in England, yes?'

'No. It's a different country. Like Scotland and Ireland, Wales is a different country to England.'

'Oh...'

Abroad – Mexico

'Where are you from?'

'Wales.'

'Where?'

'Wales. In the UK.'

'UK, oh, in England.'

'NO! Next door to England.'

'Like London?'

'No, London is in England. It's the capital. Our capital is Cardiff.'

'Like Manchester and Liverpool?'

'They're English cities. It's over the bridge from Bristol... Cymru, Gales?'

'De Galles? In France?!'

'No, in the UK, next to England.'

'So belonging to England?'

'NO! England, Scotland, Ireland...'

'Ah yes, Scotland!'

'You're joking? You know Scotland and major English cities but you've never heard of Wales?'

'...Can you write it down for me?'

And so it goes. The last exchange was developed from Americans asking which side of the wall I lived on. Assuming they meant Hadrian's, I began to explain, only to find they were *Game of Thrones* fans who believed the show to be factually based on British accents and also geographically accurate. If I had to explain that the lands of Westeros were a work of fiction by a pensioner from New Jersey, what hope did I have of explaining the land of my fathers? But, using popular culture as a compass, I tried to steer them in the right direction.

'*You know Tom Jones?*'

'Yeah! Woooaaah, Huuuh!!'

'*That's it! Where he's from.*'

'California...?'

'*What? No, Wales. Catherine Zeta-Jones? Anthony Hopkins? Where they're from.*'

'Sir, they're also from California.'

'*They're from Treforest, Swansea and Margam, butt.*'

It was hopeless.

I've drawn countless maps of Great Britain in condensation on windows and on serviettes in restaurants, from the tip of the Scottish Isles to the home counties, the arse end of England to the pregnant bulge of Wales above Devon and Cornwall. But it turns out Wales is a stillborn nation, a forgotten growth, a disfigured limb collecting water for England. A mass of land absorbed into mainland Britain, to foreigners at least. Fifteen years after devolution and the birth of the National Assembly, yet we're still considered the Principality. This was recently highlighted in the commentary of the 2014 Commonwealth Games' opening ceremony by none other than Huw Edwards – journalist and lead presenter of BBC News, Welsh speaker, son of a prolific Welsh historian and narrator of the celebrated *Story of Wales* series, who sat idly by as his co-presenter, Hazel

Irvine, referred to Wales as 'the Principality' to an audience of millions. Wales won't get anywhere if one of our prominent public figures forgets how to define it.

But I don't blame him.

I consider myself politically-engaged, relatively knowledgable about Wales and how it's governed, yet ashamedly, I found out that the Welsh Assembly and the Welsh Government are not the same thing due to a recent episode of *Question Time*. But I didn't find this out through the TV programme. Like 41% of UK adults, I found this information on the internet[1] and like 40% of its users who use social media for news[2], I found this piece of information on Twitter. Specifically in a retweet notification from a friend who worked in the Welsh Assembly building, the Senedd. The tweet stated that since the panel didn't have a single Welsh Assembly Member amongst them, only Members of Parliament, it was no wonder they kept getting facts wrong and it was apparent that none of the panelists knew the difference either. With mock keypad rage, I retweeted. Then I realised two things which led to the foundations of this essay:

(A) I wasn't watching said episode of *Question Time*, I was in bed reading *Stiffs*, a comic about apocalyptic zombie hunters in the South Wales Valleys.

(B) I was outraged that English MPs didn't know facts about Wales that I didn't actually know myself. I undid the retweet and attempted to analyse my hypocrisy.

Was this unknown fact a fault of my own? After all, as I said, I kept abreast of Welsh affairs, via media: social, digital and periodicals. I'd met my MP and AM a number of times, knew they served the same party, were based in the same local party office but worked in two different cities, Cardiff and Westminster. So how didn't I know that the *Welsh Assembly* and *Welsh Government* were different? I posted a status and tweeted and

---

[1] http://stakeholders.ofcom.org.uk/binaries/research/tv-research/news/2014/News_Report_2014.pdf

[2] http://www.rosemcgrory.co.uk/2014/01/06/uk-social-media-statistics-for-2014/

then I visited the local café and library and asked the same question. The replies I received were as I originally thought..

Not many people did know.

How didn't they know? Was it because they hadn't been told or because people couldn't actually tell the difference who governed what? Or was it far simpler, that very few of them cared?

Most knew one thing: that Wales's headquarters was in Cardiff Bay because Cardiff Bay is always in the background of the news on BBC Wales and ITV Wales. Because that tiny pocket of the Welsh capital is always being discussed and is recognisable on telly. It has everything crammed into it: Culture, Tourism, Power and parking meters. It has the big red Pierhead building, which some I spoke to thought *was* the Senedd. It has the grand slate, copper and timber clad Wales Millennium Centre, which many thought was *attached* to the Senedd somehow. Only a handful recognised that it was actually the building next door. Impressive with its wooden curves, sleek glass and slate floors, people could recognise it in the architectural cluster of the bay but not many could name it in isolation (many on Pinterest thought it was a nature-based building because it looked like a giant mushroom). So technically, they had locality spot on, CF99, but in terms of recognising its powers, or rather the limitations of its powers, there's the rub. What good is recognition of *where* governs us if you cannot name *what* it governs?

I later found out that it's enough for those who work there.

I read a part of this essay at the Made in Roath festival in 2014, where an older man sat in the corner of the tea room in a trench coat like someone from a Graham Greene novel. After I finished reading, he leant over from his seat under the stairs to tell me I was wrong. The following exchange took place:

'I think you'll find that a lot of people know the difference,' he attempted to correct me.

'Well, I've spoken to a lot of different people, in south Wales at least, and not many of them do. Did you two know?' I asked my sister-in-law, a solicitor, and my wife, who works for the council. Both said that they weren't totally sure what the difference was.

'Well, I can assure you that the people who *need* to know, know the difference.'

All three of us were taken aback at his brazen remark.

'The ones who need to know?! So the people of the country that elected them don't *need* to know what powers they have over them?!' I asked.

At this point a cluster of the audience came to speak to me to share the same view. They didn't know the difference nor what the circumstantial powers of the Welsh Assembly were compared to the Welsh Government.

'Well I'm one of the health ministers and I can tell you that many people *know* that health is devolved in Wales, at least,' he mumbled dismissively, wrapping a scarf around his neck and making his way towards the exit.

This man worked in the very institution I was challenging to define itself and not only couldn't he do so, he refused to even accept the fact of a conflicting opinion! We weren't playing devil's advocate by dismissing his claim in the existence of Santa or UFOs. I was stating facts about the people of Wales' political unfamiliarity backed up by these very people who happened to agree with me. I didn't know which minister he was or what in the health department he was in charge of but I'm sure those who *needed* to know, did.

It began to make a little more sense. If those that work at the Senedd assure themselves enough that those who 'need to know', as the minister insightfully put it, know, then the rest is water under the Severn Bridge. Were they happy to crack on with things until the political shit hit the fan hoping that nobody knew said shit was devolved? Ironically, a few weeks after that reading, the NHS in Wales came under fire because it was not hitting targets. The Tories began to use it as fuel for their attacks on Labour in preparation for the following year's general election. Did the Senedd think that some laypeople of Wales would blame the Tory cabinet ministers, Andrew Lansley or Jeremy Hunt, hoping they didn't know that health had been devolved in 1999 when the National Assembly of Wales was established? Teachers loved to bash the controversial and educationally malignant Michael Gove, but from my discussions, it was predominantly educational workers that knew it was my own constituency's AM, Leighton Andrews, who was in charge of Education in Wales during Gove's tenure. Others still assumed it was Michael Gove.

There may not be more than hope for Wales' engagement with its own governance if it's happy to govern in a collective ignorance, but outside of politics and outside of Wales, could *some* collective ignorance, projected in the right way, help establish a broader sense of international recognition?

Braveheart and *Michael Collins* are both films about important and significant battles for independence and/or political freedoms from oppressive English rule over Celtic nations. Neil Patrick Jordan promoted Ireland and Mel Gibson promoted Scotland. There have been much finer films on the same topic since, notably *Hunger* and *The Wind that Shakes the Barley*, but these two released within a year of each other in the mid-1990s stand out for two particular reasons. Both films did well in the box office worldwide, one was nominated for and the other won Academy Awards. Both also play fast and loose with facts about the leading characters for cinematic purposes while introducing historical events of small European countries to a wider audience.

So I propose that the Welsh Assembly send out-to-tender an invite for a producer/director to do the same for Wales. Facts aside. Just a good old-fashioned bums-on-seats box-office blockbuster based on Welsh events to promote the country('s historical struggles) to the world.

We are a nation of clans and infighting, whether it's lands and leaders, regions and religions, sports or politics, there are rivalries everywhere. It could even be Mel again since he did the same for the Mayans with *Apocalypto*. Throwing facts in to the sacrificial cenote for a good story that inspired tourists to flood to Mexico to visit Mayan ruins such as Chichen Itza, Mayapan and Uxmal.

To dramatise *Braveheart* into a three-hour film, Mel may have tinkered with the chronology of his facts (Isabelle of France would have been 9 years old when William Wallace supposedly had it off with her) and amended the costumes (kilts weren't worn by men until centuries after the famous battle of Stirling and had stopped painting their faces centuries prior). But at least he still based it on actual historical facts, unlike Iolo Morgannwg.

Iolo Morgannwg was a Welsh poet, collector and ultimately a forger of an entire culture. His lasting legacy is that he fabricated the entire foundation of what is now an internationally-renowned cultural institution, the Gorsedd of the Bards at the National Eisteddfod of Wales. He 'reenacted' a basic ritual with his bardic butties, claiming that it was a long-held tradition of the druids, which he proceeded to perform with some forged props on June 21, 1792 on Primrose Hill, in London (of all places!). Twenty-seven years later, in 1819, it became part of the Eisteddfod at the Ivy Bush Inn in Carmarthen. The National Eisteddfod was established in Aberdare in 1861. It now has around 150,000 visitors for the annual week-long event in August bringing in £6–8 million to the local economy of each area it visits[3]. This already beats the Wallace Monument in Sterling which has around 130,000 international visitors a year[4]. The Eisteddfod's international equivalent at Llangollen welcomes around 36,000 visitors to the town every year, bringing £1.5 million to the local area.

---

[3] http://www.eisteddfod.org.uk/english/about-us/the-eisteddfod/supporting-the-economy/

[4] http://www.bbc.co.uk/news/uk-scotland-tayside-central-13896765

So if Mel can draw visitors to Sterling in Scotland with a screenplay and some face-paint and Iolo can do it with some forged sticks and a few pebbles in a circle, then surely somebody can harness the same ingenuity to project Wales to the world in 90–180 minutes of digital celluloid?

The last film that did anything near this and is held dear to the heart of most Welsh people who've watched it describes a story similar to William Wallace's beginnings, the plight of two impoverished Welshmen who seek vengeance after the brutal murder of their family. Unfortunately the 1997 cult film *Twin Town* did not receive such worldwide recognition as *Braveheart* did two years prior, but this could be down to the fact that Michael Collins and William Wallace sought vengeance against the *English*, whereas the Lewis 'twins' ultimately sought retribution against a *Welsh* drug baron and a *Scottish* bent copper. Infighting again. The film was also made by a Welshman, Kevin Allen. What we need is a Welsh story to capture the imagination and a foreign director to widen the field for respectability and recognition.

Once a year, the Prince of Monaco hosts the Monaco Wales Association's St David's Day luncheon based on all things Welsh[5], attended by cultural and sporting Welsh royalty[6]. Apparently, Prince Albert II befriended a Welshman who taught him *Sosban Fach* and has been an avid fan of Welsh Rugby ever since. If a seemingly innocuous little sing song about a harassed Welsh housewife's daily troubles, adopted by a local rugby club as its unofficial anthem, sung on a drunken night out could inspire a foreign monarch to throw an annual event at the Hotel de Paris in Monte Carlo, then a successful cinematic equivalent could yield endless possibilities.

On this same first day in March, the Empire State Building projected red, white and

---

[5] http://maboum.com/event-10486

[6] http://www.walesonline.co.uk/news/wales-news/prince-monaco-joins-dame-shirley-1843477

green lights into the New York skyline[7] to celebrate the 'forgotten' Welsh connection to America's Declaration of Independence, of which 18 of the 56 co-signatories were of Welsh origin. One of these founding fathers', Francis Lewis, birthplace is stated as Llandaff, Wales on the declaration itself[8]. But the Welsh don't dye their beer green on St David's Day and a harp is a lot harder to carry in a parade so the St Patrick's Day on the 17th of March still holds more precedence than the 1st in the US of A.

Lewis' story is an interesting one for screenplay. His wife was captured and subsequently died from the cruel conditions while she was imprisoned by the English[9]. He was a Welsh speaker who managed to evade captivity from Native Americans through navigating the linguistics of his captors via Welsh linguistic traits. He *did* battle for independence against the English, albeit on the wrong side of the pond. It could even be pitched as an emigration story to New York but would be difficult to pull off since *The Godfather Part II* is THE emigration story of them all.

There are many other historical figures that are inevitably entwined with Wales' battles for independence: for example, Llewelyn ap Gruffudd aka Llewelyn ein Llyw olaf or Llywelyn the Last, known for his battlefield conquests against various English kings. However, his story would be marred by the fact that he made a number of concessions to those same English kings, contrasting with unyielding, uncompromising Celtic rebels such as Collins and Wallace. Also, minor Welsh leaders of the time, particularly the princes of south Wales kept rebelling against him, so once more, notorious in-fighting amongst the Welsh rears its ugly head. Finally, his death is mired in controversy and conspiracy, with some reports saying he was slain in battle after being duped and

---

[7] http://www.nbcnews.com/id/7044972/ns/world_news/t/welsh-often-overlooked-make-their-case/#.VddC99NVhHw

[8] http://www.ushistory.org/declaration/signers/lewis.htm

[9] http://www.dsdi1776.com/signers-by-state/francis-lewis/

separated from his army while others claiming he was killed by a lone lancer while travelling back to them. Either way, both accounts describe him as being tricked and then killed, the future of Wales as a free country dying along with him. Whichever way the scriptwriter frames it, it's not much of a battle cry for us, 800 years after the fact.

Owain Glyndwr is a legend in Welsh folklore as the last man to legitimately hold the title of Prince of Wales and his credence in inspiring Wales to take up arms to reclaim the country from English rule would make a fine film. He was also a rebel and despite enormous rewards being offered, he was never captured and ignored royal pardons even after disappearance in 1412. He is named as the father of Welsh Nationalism for his uncompromising stance with a number of groups, some controversially, adopting his symbolism to advocate for independence. Recent resurrections by the Assembly celebrated the 600th anniversary of his revolt in 2000 and subsequent stamps, statues and newly-established universities also tie him back in to modern Wales. But like Llewelyn, his death is unclear due to his disappearance and supposed death four years later, so again a headache for scriptwriters who need a pay off before the closing credits.

One Welshman fits the mould. A socio-political giant and working-class hero who is entrenched in current affairs not because he was a prominently controversial public figure in his day but purely because he is the father of his still contentiously debated creation. Someone who was born and bred in poverty in the South Wales Valleys. Someone who built a career based on a drive to serve those who he saw as struggling unnecessarily due to their social situation, what he considered inhumane living conditions, something that was a fundamental right. He fought for social justice and to reform the welfare state so that the people of his own community and eventually the whole of Britain across the ages deserved to be treated equally, regardless of income or social standing. His principles and determination built his greatest accomplishment and he would become an inspirational figure in Wales, enough to be voted number one in a list of the 100 Welsh Heroes[10] by the Welsh public.

> 'The collective principle asserts that... no society can legitimately call itself civilised if denied medical aid because of lack of means.'

Aneurin Bevan, a Welshman, established the National Health Service.

Now if Iolo Morgannwg, a poet, could get Wales culturally acknowledged by 'discovering' something that ancient Welsh druids supposedly practiced and making the rest up as he went along then maybe another Welsh poet could 'discover' something new about Nye Bevan. The poet Owen Sheers wrote *Resistance*, a novel which subsequently was made into a film, about an alternative history where the Nazis successfully invade Britain. Michael Sheen performed a modern day reenactment of the story of the crucifixion in front of the people of Port Talbot in *The Gospel of Us* written by Owen Sheers. Maybe the Arts Council of Wales could fund a grant scheme for an established writer to write a screenplay for an established director to direct an established film on the founder of the NHS?

This is not an original idea. One film has been made of the great man. Trevor Griffiths, an Englishman of Irish and Welsh descent, wrote and directed *Food for Ravens* for the BBC in 1997. A poignant eulogy of an ailing Bevan looking back on his life from a hospital bed. Bevan was played by the Scotsman Brian Cox and his wife played by the Irish actress, Sinéad Cusack. It was critically acclaimed and won the Royal Television Society award for Best Regional Programme 1997 and the Gwyn A Williams award at the Welsh BAFTAs. But it was refused funding by BBC Network for being 'too recherché for the film audiences targeted by the

---

[10] http://www.100welshheroes.com/en/biography/aneurinbevan

Network[11], and after finally being made as a film for television was snuck out on BBC Wales at 23:15 on a Sunday night with no fanfare and barely a whisper of advertising. It just goes to show that like the NHS, something great can become a great waste in the wrong hands.

Mark Thomson, BBC2 controller at the time, claimed it was only being filmed for the benefit of Wales and David Thomson, Head of BBC films, added that, 'You'd need a degree in political science to know what was going on.' A biopic of a notorious politician looking back on their lives, from simple upbringing to politicisation and finally power-houses in government, from the narrative of a frail old age and illness? If only Meryl Streep was given this screenplay in 1997 instead of taking the lead in ...*First Do No Harm*, a film for television of one woman's struggle against a narrow-minded medical establishment. Irony is a string of pearls.

So if the narrative of a politician's biopic is too difficult or too cliché for modern-day audiences then an alternative needs to be pitched.

Plot: A binder has been found in the annals of St Fagans Welsh Folk Museum with files of Aneurin Bevan's long-lost plans with hidden instructions if anyone ever attempted to dismantle and sell off the National Health Service. A secret clause reveals that any signatory of a sitting government that willingly privatised or abolished the service would be imprisoned based on laws tantamount to treason. Similar to burying the fact that the Tory chancellor, George Osbourne, borrowed more in the 2010–15 administration than every Labour government put together, the Tories attempt to keep the clause hidden from the public and the press, particularly the *Guardian*. But the 'Vermin' clause is enforced by the spirit of Bevan, sent in the form of a robot so he can pass undetected with modern-day politicians. Part political drama, part sci-fi action extravaganza.

---

[11] https://www.closeupfilmcentre.com/vertigo_magazine/volume-1-issue-8-summer-1998/food-for-ravens/

Title:	*Vermin: A Political Terminator from Tredegar*
Tagline:	'He'll put them in a hospital... that he founded.'
Sequels:	*Vermin II: Nye v. Maggie* – The Tories recreate a bionic Margaret Thatcher in an attempt to stop any reform.
	Vermin III: Origins – Return to Tredegar to show the emergence of Nye from humble beginnings as a 'troublemaker' trade union rep to his political heights as deputy leader of the Labour party... Basically a reboot of *Food for Ravens*.

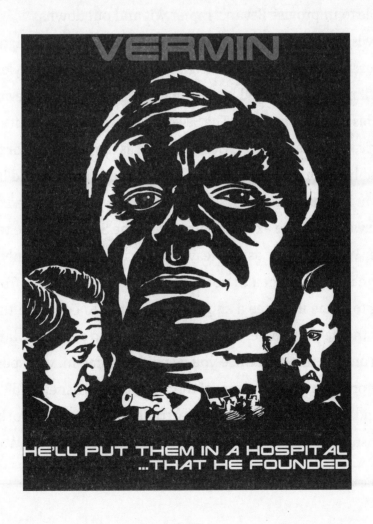

Michael Sheen has already played one saviour and unfortunately portrayed the most notorious modern-day British politician, Tony Blair, not once but three times in *The Deal*, *The Queen* and *The Special Relationship*. Matthew Rhys has recently played another Welsh icon, Dylan Thomas, and Rhys Ifans, as prolific an actor as he is, is far too thin. Welsh casting agents would probably go for a beloved cast member of *Pobl y Cwm*, so they need to be bypassed to punt for a superstar actor who could dedicate time and effort to emulate the distinct oratory style and deacon-esque delivery of his speeches as well as being able to improvise Bevan's rapier wit and put downs.

Daniel Day-Lewis would spend six months in Tredegar putting on weight, throwing darts at pictures of Churchill and learning the accent in true method actor's style. Like Sheen's *The Gospel of Us*, the film would be played in real time at Tredegar, where Bevan made his inaugural speech for his plans for the NHS. The Seven Bridge toll, given that it's near parity with the admission price of a cinema ticket, would be used as the box office for the performance.

In terms of publicity, premiering in 2018, the M4 speed limit would be raised from 15 mph to 70 mph in honour of the years since the NHS was established. This would also draw attention away from the extortionate rate of the Severn Bridge toll which is only paid as you enter Wales and not as you leave, which ironically can only be levied by the Secretary of State in Parliament and not beyond its tolls in Cardiff[12]. Tourists, believing they are paying to come in to see a show, would begin to compare the experience to entering a giant theme park. Where else attracts you into a magical land full of castles and stereotypes only to find that once you've paid to come in, you spend most of your time queuing before even getting to any of the attractions? Disneyland? The irony being, unlike Disneyland, none of the 'entrance fee' comes to those who work this side of the gates, but like Disneyland Paris, a percentage does go to the French. Wales doesn't get a

---

[12] http://www.legislation.gov.uk/ukpga/1992/3/contents

penny. The tolls collected by Severn Bridge Crossing Plc, owned by English and French building companies with British and American investment banks[13] who have until 2017 to collect the concessions for building the bridge before they have to return the toll to maintenance costs[14] instead of reaping £52 million a year. Poor dabs.

A Welsh Government survey suggested that if the tolls were removed then 22% of tourists living in south-west England would be more likely to make a trip to Wales within the next year[15]. This number is estimated to raise significantly if an Irish actor playing a Welsh politician performed a three-hour soliloquy on the inevitable destruction of the NHS at the hands of the English ruling class party.

All those entering via the Heads of the Valley road past Ebbw Vale to Tredegar with the options of travelling further to Rhymney, Merthyr Tydfil, Hirwaun and Glynneath, would be given a free tour of Welsh cultural, geographical and industrial heritage along the way as a prelude to the show. Separate Valley safari trips could be purchased in advance to visit sites such as the Chartists caves, Tower Colliery, Cyfartha Castle, Merthyr viaduct, or the big Asda at Dowlais top, with views of the Black Mountains, the Brecon Beacons National Park and Pen y Cymoedd, the largest onshore windfarm in Western Europe. Past, present and future in one car journey all before arriving at their destination for a *Western Mail* 5-star-reviewed Eisteddfod of emotions in live performance.

Once the final credit has rolled, the audience will erupt in applause, weeping with raw emotion at what they've witnessed in a small town in the heart of the Welsh Valleys. As they leave they'll get an additional real-life epilogue from modern Wales. They'll see

---

[13] http://www.morningstar.co.uk/uk/News/NewsFeedItem.aspx?id=200413911481744

[14] http://www.publications.parliament.uk/pa/cm201011/cmselect/cmwelaf/506/10110402.htm

[15] http://gov.wales/docs/caecd/research/121105severntollsfinalen.pdf

that no matter how much of himself Bevan put into securing the future of the NHS because of the degradation and the penury of his community in Tredegar, apart from a free health service, not much has actually changed. Ushered through the rain by locals in high-vis jackets, they'll drive back to where they came from in single file, staring out of the windows at the boarded-up shops, the lack of industry, lack of employment, lack of council services, lack of enthusiasm and dying post-industrial communities. They'll see the anger and the vitriol which fuelled the screenplay and, with the performance still fresh in their minds, they will drive home. As they sit quietly, in air-conditioned contemplation, they'll feel they've been completely immersed in what Wales really is, an angry nation shouting across at those that oppose them in the hope of saving and sustaining what they hold dear. Hopefully, after about a year, those same audience members will feel the need to experience those emotions again and buy the DVD with making-of extras and interviews with the professional and community cast and crew for a discounted price from Amazon.

Progressively it's the wrong shaped ball that has done more for Wales' global standings since writing this essay. Wales' Euro 2016 football team progressed further than they ever imagined in an internationally renowned tournament that preceded a vote on whether Britain should remain or leave the European Union. Who'd have thought that a game with such appalling social history of hooliganism and racism, from both sides of the bridge, could foster such a hopeful enthusiasm from a continent that Wales, along with England, had only weeks prior turned its back on? Welsh fans, brass bands and choirs alike were welcomed, encouraged and applauded for their positivity in the throes of (what ultimately proved to be) a referendum's negativity towards foreigners, be it on or off the field, in cafés or tea rooms, in hospitality or penalty boxes. Wales announced itself on the world's stage and was finally recognised as separate to England.

More than that, for the first time in over half a century they were proven to be better, throughout the tournament, as a team and as humbled, fun loving, law abiding supporters. England may have bore the brunt of the foreign media's negative coverage but, sadly, from a political standpoint Wales stood arm in arm with the 52% that voted out of the European Union. But sport's national buoyancy in the midst of a storm can be confusing when our inclusion in Euro 2016 alone was cause for celebration, while both exits from Europe will undoubtedly lead us down two very different paths.

In 2014, the NATO Summit came to Wales and effectively closed down two of its major cities, Newport and Cardiff. Wales, like any nation with a spotlight on them for a while, became very excited and, eventually, very annoyed at being centre stage. We watched 180 VIPs, 4,000 delegates and officials from over 60 countries use Wales as the stage to promote their own countries. As with most stages, only the performers get to be on it, not the plebs in the stalls. It was heralded as the most important summit since the fall of the Berlin Wall yet was criticised for being devoid of any political perspectives. Cardiff Castle was illuminated behind the world leaders as the curtains closed on the summit. It was a beautifully framed shot that showed the unique location of the summit. But it wasn't Carwyn Jones of Cardiff, Wales that people saw in the photo. It was David Cameron of London, England. Where was that summit with the castle again...? Politics may not be the platform to project modern Wales, since we are still the understudies of our own governance. A third-act crescendo of independence is still a far cry from any sort of script, let alone a standing ovation.

THEY'RE INBRED, PAMPERED AND COST A FORTUNE TO KEEP...

BUT PARADE THEM IN FRONT OF MILLIONS ONCE A YEAR...

AND THE PUBLIC CAN'T GET ENOUGH OF THEM!

©SIÔNMUN

Also Elizabeth

In 1946
In the hope of creating a more common link with Wales,
Princess Elizabeth
Was inducted to the Welsh Gorsedd of Bards
At the National Eisteddfod
Held at Mountain Ash
In the Cynon Valley.

A stone's throw away,
At Pontypridd Registry Office,
My grandmother,
Also Elizabeth,
Married my grandfather,
Who was not 6ft 1 or of Greek descent
But 5ft 3 and from Treharne Street, Pentre,
In the Rhondda Valley.

But like Phillip,
Tommy served in the Navy, 1939–1945,
And as 'Lillibet' joined the Auxiliary Territorial Service,
Betty 'painted bullets' at Bridgend Arsenal.

In 1952
Elizabeth Windsor
Was told of her father's death by her husband
At the Treetops Hotel, Segana Lodge, Kenya.
Elizabeth Owen
Was told of her father's death by her husband
In the lean-to kitchen of their terraced house
In number 13 Upper Alma Place, Pentre, south Wales.

On her 21st birthday
The future Queen Elizabeth Alexandra Mary,
In a public appearance, said,
'I declare before you all that my whole life,
Whether it be long or short,
Shall be devoted to your service'.

From 1952 until 2012
Queen Elizabeth II
Fulfilled her duty for sixty years
As the second-longest reigning British monarch
Along with the Duke of Edinburgh,
As the longest serving consort to a Queen regent.

On his 21ˢᵗ birthday
My father's uncle Emlyn
Suffered a severe attack of Meningitis.
He survived but with limited capacity
And would have to be fed, bathed and cared for
His whole life.

My grandmother,
Never made a public speech.
She never made a declaration.
Emlyn was her brother.
From 1939 until 1985
She devoted forty-six years of her life to caring for him.
No one lined the streets to cheer for her.

In 1986
My grandparents celebrated
their Ruby Wedding anniversary.
The first they'd ever spent as a couple.

Every Cloud

My parents were old when they had me but that didn't matter, really, 'cause they died when I wasn't even one. My uncle took me on, my father's brother. He was always my uncle even though I don't remember my parents. Could easily have told me that he was my father, but he was always straight with me.

'Your parents died in an accident when you were little.'

'I know.'

'Then you came to stay with me.'

''Cause no one was left to look after me'

'Aye.'

''Cause you're my uncle.'

''Cause I'm your uncle.'

If I ever had a question, he'd always give me an answer that made sense. I never needed to ask for the explanation again. Only once I remember asking him twice.

He came home one day, sweating and stinking. He didn't take his boots off at the door nor throw his shirt in the passage to wash. His breath was heavy, not from the slog of a hard day but instead, from something that made him far more weary. He sat down at the small kitchen table, leaning forward in the chair while smoothing his thick black moustache. His lank hair clung to his forehead like wet leaves to a rock. He lifted his eyes to me, all pupil and full of things he wished he could wash away.

'Boy, Mr Hughes had an accident and he's dead now,' he said.

I looked at his giant hands, dirty and stained the same red as the clay on his boots. 'How d'you mean?' I asked.

'Like your parents had an accident and died, Mr Hughes has had an accident and died.

He was working on that shed at the bottom of his garden. He was digging and a sink hole opened up underneath him and swallowed him into the ground. It happens sometimes, but all his tools and a tonne of gravel fell in on top of him, like when all the bits of muck at the bottom of the bath get sucked down the plughole,' he raised his eyebrows at me to make sure I understood.

I nodded.

'Me and Dewi heard the noise and jumped over the fence to help Howard, who was already trying to get him out. We were there for 'bout half an hour before the ambulance came but by the time we got to him Mr Hughes wasn't there no more, only his body.'

He stared at me a while before signalling me over. He held me by the shoulders, his arms like hills rolling up towards his chest. He pushed his moustache out and his face softened, 'Do you understand?'

I understood what had happened to Mr Hughes but still asked.

'So it was the same with Mam and Dad's accident?'

His hands felt heavier on me, his brow furrowed as he looked down and sighed through his nose. 'Not exactly, boy,' he paused and looked over to where he was trying to remember. 'Nobody was there to try to help them so they had to die together on their own.'

He let his hands drop and sat back in the chair before saying something that I remember as vividly as the night he said it, something which would inevitably be what we'd all come to live by.

'When things happen, It affects everyone different. There's some feelings that you got to try to forget. Try your hardest, but the main thing you got to remember is: you can't ever stop some things from happening.'

He stared into me to make sure I was taking this in.

'What happened to your parents is one of those feelings, okay?'

'Okay.' I thought I knew what he meant, But I never really knew until much later on, when we would all have to endure the same thing.

Sometimes the rain beats down like buggery on the roof. A torrential attack from the sky. Like someone is trying to smash into the house. Like police used to do on telly, when people were hiding some bollocks or other, drugs usually, or poor sods that weren't supposed to be in them dosshouses. Then all the neighbours'd be outside shouting at the police or curtain twitching 'cause they knew the people in them houses were bad eggs. You'd see them jawing into the camera then, 'The roof never had snow on it 'cause they must have had them special lamps to grow it all in the attic,' and, 'I can't believe it's happened round here 'cause this is a lovely street apart from them lot.' Strange to think about that now, neighbours and drugs and telly, let alone police.

Half of the roof tiles are all to pot now but it's not like I can just pop down the builders' yard to order some new ones and get them delivered, so I got to make do with patching it up with wooden shingles and notches. I tell you, if there was anything like it still around, I'd be working for the Heritage commission. They all wanted traditional in the old days, 'green carpentry' they called it. Making things all natural. Normal it is now though, 'cause we can't do bugger all else. There's no one making anything anymore unless you're making it yourself.

When we used to do hobbles and they'd ask if we could do something like split log shingles or limestone plastering, we'd say, 'Aye, course we can!', charge 'em double, then google it when we got home to learn how to do it. The old boys used to do the same only it'd take them longer to learn cause they'd have to get the books from the library. I remember showing them a video on my phone and they'd say, 'Dur, technology's marvellous.' Little did them old boys know. Now there's still libraries around, dusty books on shelves in smashed-up buildings, unless they've been burned, but Google...?

I'm sure it never used to rain this hard before. Course it *rained*, but it was all sorts; windy rain, fat rain, mental rain, that shitty little rain that doesn't actually feel like it's raining but you're wet when you get home. But since it happened, it's like the raindrops got bigger and when you get caught in it it's like being smacked on the nut, like the sky hates you and pelts you 'till you find cover. At night it's like it's trying to keep the world awake to tell us that we fucked it all up.

But at least it's not acid rain like everyone was shitting themselves about. After all them colours and the thunder and lightning, they were ranting that we'd all have it coming. Screaming about the loss of crops and it all going to hell and everyone was going to starve 'cause things were going to go toxic or melt. And it was all bollocks. Bloody lies to scare everyone. Some poor buggers even tried to burn everything to 'Save the Crops.' Caused absolute chaos 'cause of the media that couldn't get enough of it. 10% disaster, 90% hysteria. Still trying to sell papers and make money when eventually that sort of nonsense wouldn't even matter anymore. Useless. Bullshit the lot of it. Well, the hysteria not the disaster...

But I never used to read the papers.

The morning after it happened, she had a go at me for not 'keeping up' with it.

'It's important,' she said.

'I know it is,' It wasn't that I weren't reading about it, it's just that I knew there wouldn't be any answers from them.

'We need to know what's going on.'

'I know what's going on, I've got eyes haven't I!?'

She widened hers when I said this, because it's exactly what I used to say to her when she'd try to talk to me in the pictures. She'd *cwtch* down onto my arm and share popcorn through the adverts, saying which films she wanted to see and which actors were on our 'laminated Five', which were five celebrities we'd allow each other to have it off with, if by some ridiculous circumstance they ended up down our local. Then as soon as the film would start, everyone would settle down to watch and within five minutes, she'd start asking questions; 'Who's that?', 'What's he doing now?', 'Why is she going in there?'. I'd always say 'You got eyes haven't you? I'm watching the same film as you.' Then she'd move to the other side of her seat to pout for a while before coming back over when she got cold or wanted popcorn. She always came back.

'I mean what caused it. How it happened. How we can stop it happening again...'

'Stop it happening again? Have you looked outside?! See that sky?!' I threw the curtains open like I was revealing a terrifying work of art. 'It's not going to happen again! Bugger all is going to happen again! They're not going to tell us how it happened 'cause the people who know what happened are never going to come out again. They've disappeared away from all this! Somewhere where they think they're safe from whatever *this* is.' I picked up the paper and held up the famous picture that was on the cover of everything. The Kodak moment of our fate, 'And this bullshit will be the last fucking thing we'll see to remember it all! How everything used to be, 'cause it's never going to be the same after this, sweetheart...'

I was still ranting at the sky, then I turned round and saw her face. Welling up, again. She hadn't stopped since it happened. It affects everyone different. Sometimes I watch her when she sleeps. She doesn't know obviously, cause she's kipping hard. When you don't see other people often, I'm talking months on end, you'd think you'd be bored to tears of seeing the same face. But at night, when I roll over and catch the side of her cheek in whatever light's coming through the window, moonlight usually, but not like romantic bollocks, just light shining through the curtains, she's beautiful. I don't know if it's because she's sleeping, she doesn't have to worry about anything, but when she's just lying there, head on the pillow and I can see her chest going up and down as she's breathing, she just looks peaceful. Her eyes look softer, less harsh and her lips curl up a bit so it's almost like she's smiling, like she knows I'm watching her. But the night it happened and the sky changed and for that brief moment her face was illuminated with the most terrible white light, she never looked more beautiful and she's never looked the same.

'Oi, don't now. None of that. Pointless. We're buggered and now we got to get on with it.'

She turned away and wiped the tears from her cheeks.

I picked up my phone to try ringing my uncle again. I'd been trying all morning. Nothing, just endless dial-tone. 'How hard it is to record a bloody voicemail?'

She grabbed her coat and bag from the chair. 'I got to see Mam and Dad. You know how Dad's going to be with all this. I told you, when they showed it on the news the first time, he started cleaning his rifle and polishing his boots. He thinks it's war again. He doesn't know what he's doing.'

'Nobody does!'

'Mam won't be able to deal with him on her own.'

'They're saying not to go outside. Ain't you listening to the papers?'

She gave me a look that was all I needed to know.

'When you coming back?' I don't know why I asked. I already knew.

'Dunnow,' and she shut the door behind her.

There's Ending and then there's Endurance. Both hard to deal with. Both are lonely. Both leave someone behind. Both are eventually realised before they can be understood. She left them both where she found them. There was a notepad and pen on the table next to where her father sat, but he never wrote a word. Her mother had been drinking tea by the window and her father had just finished polishing his boots. He knew what he was doing.

For some reason she took the rifle, like she thought it might prevent anything worse from happening.

I kept trying my uncle.

My uncle was a tough old bloke. He was forced to retire after the bucket of a JCB clouted him and he fell off a scaffold. I remember hearing the bang and running over seeing a plume of dust rising above where he'd landed. Thought it had killed him but it didn't. He pulled through but he weren't right after that.

He wasn't a storyteller but he chose his words carefully when he explained things and he never lied. But after his accident, his words would be all over the shop. One day, 'He'd be fine' and the next, 'Hebde efni'. Apart from his garbled words you wouldn't even know anything was wrong, but when his words failed him, he'd get frustrated. The doctors said that he'd need anger management since it was a side effect of a bang on the head; forgetfulness, rages and obsessive behaviour. I never really saw him lose his temper much before, but after it, he'd get angry at the daftest things. I arrived one day and he was livid, pacing back and forth, the TV remote sticking out of the telly. 'That prick on there said the world's going to end if we carry on,' he shouted pointing at the smashed screen, standing in his dressing gown, spittle on his moustache. 'And I'm not bloody having that!' He stood panting like a dog, not realising what he looked like until later, when he'd put his head in his hands and start rubbing his temples as if trying to wipe out the memories. Trying his hardest. Broke my bloody heart seeing him like that.

Took about two years for him to get proper better. Iron out the bits of bonkers that would pop out now and again as a reminder of the bang. Walking helped the most. He'd get the exercise he missed from work and he'd be knackered enough when he got home that he felt like he'd done something. And he loved the scenery. He'd say, 'You should see some of the views we've got, mun. I've lived here all my life and I never even knew. If it weren't for that bang on the head I could have died without seeing them.' It turned into a good thing.

But with it came the obsessiveness. He began walking up to the same spot every day, up to the labyrinthine mazes of the forestry roads. He could walk for hours up there and get a new view of a different valley in every which way he chose. Miles and miles. Claimed he could even see down to the coast through some of the clearings in the trees.

He left at daft o'clock each morning with his sandwiches and a flask of tea in his coat pocket. He used to wander but he began spending more and more time at the locked entrance to the old tunnel that used to go all the way through to the other valley. They shut it over half a century ago and shuttered it up with cladding but then kids used to go up there, break bits off and try to see how deep it would go. Inevitably something went wrong and two kids died after going in after dark. They put up huge iron gates after that and bolted them shut.

I came home one day and his eyes were wild. He was beaming and confused like a kid who still believed in Father Christmas but had found his presents under his parents' bed. He kept saying that he'd seen a council van go up to the gates. A bloke got out with a clipboard and a set of keys. He said that the bloke opened the gates and looked inside as if there was something in there that he didn't want to see, marking something down on his sheet before shutting the gates quick, bolting and locking it. That was it. It consumed him.

He'd stand in front of those gates for hours, wondering what was in there and after a while, his theories became wilder. He began to read about what the tunnel was. An old mine entrance that was closed after a disaster but was used to store machinery. Tracks laid for miles but after a section collapsed, it was too expensive to clear and was eventually blocked up. He'd mourn the deaths of the miners and the two boys that lost their lives inside there. He'd press his ears to the metal and listen. Then he began saying he could hear their voices through the door. Finally the conspiracy theories. The council were storing things in there, building a bunker under the mountain. Keeping people that weren't supposed to be there. Trapped or living. Hiding things from us. Why did that bloke not go in to see? Why did he look scared? What was he checking on?

'They're hiding something in there. They're preparing for something. They know something and they're not telling us!' He was lost.

That one bloke looking frightened into the darkness of that tunnel was a prophetic metaphor and the grand irony of my uncle's decline was that he would lead me to him the day after it happened.

After ringing and ringing without answer, I knew exactly where to look. They told us not to go out but I took my works mask, got up early like him and walked through the back lanes until the tarmac turned to gravel and I followed the ventricular path up towards the mountains.

As I crested the brow of the final stretch, the sun catching the frost on the rocks hulking from the mountain face, I saw him.

You try your hardest but sometimes you can't stop some things from happening.

My uncle's body lay on the ground before the gates, his face twisted in terrifying awe, his hands tight fists like he was preparing for a fight. His wild theories burning in a fireball in the distance. A flaming white light of questions that finally burned as brightly as his compulsion.

I closed his eyes.

Behind him, through the break in the forestry road, the gigantic mushroom cloud was still visible.

The Oxymoron

You are now entering

The post-industrial 'regenerated' south Wales valleys.

Reversing up through the one way out

That ebbs trudging commuters like silt

Down a bottleneck,

Wedged between two gouged, fern-compensated hills,

Rotting green and orange like week-old pumpkins.

To the hub of activity and investment

Of a city, growing in numbers,

Swept up in a mulching heap

Like leaves under the feet of those who flee

The branches of this dying tree,

Whose bark is worse than its bitemarks.

Held at arm's length from the inadvertent hand that feeds us,

Which once took as we continued to give.

Which now takes as we continue to live.

Picking at the scab of an industry,

We are amputated

And encouraged to be indebted

To the prosthetic attitude

Of the voice at the

End of the line.

A man dies clutching his phone, bleeding in the gutter, having signed his life away to an analogy between satire and futurism.

Our man stands outside his door taking in his surroundings. He sees the world going to hell: rubbish strewn in the garden, the unkempt lawn, the cracks in the pavements, and that's just his place. Others are much worse. The council are terrible. They keep blaming him, saying that as a tenant he should take care of his own home, but why should he when his taxes go towards it? He used to pay taxes all the time before they forced him on benefits and now his back has packed in too, there's no hope. Unbelievable. They're totally useless, the council, they'll have to come and do something about the state of the place soon. Looks awful. The Union Jack towel fluttering in the breeze from his bathroom window is the only thing he can take pride in. He stares across the road at those going in and out of the potholes, before cursing the council letter stapled to the lamp post:

Potholes will be dealt with in due course through ensuring the appropriate procedure is followed as is noted in the Temporary Permanent Reduction of Work Act in accordance with the Reformation Act of Local Government (2010). Future work may possibly commence before or after an allocated timescale-approved date.

Phase 1: Highlighting the documented section of weathered highway compression areas in non-lead based eco-soluble paint (BS7W47), pre-filling documented section of weathered highway compression areas with eco-primer (BSH17). Once primed period is complete, eco-filler (BS80085) to be applied to documented section of weathered highway compression areas to avoid further degradation, and finally final primer filling (BS717).

Phase 2: Post-filling may begin following an 18-month consultation period.

Locals hate the lamp post almost as much as the pothole, especially since the pre-letter letter stapled three months prior, implied the lamp post may be replaced with a permanent one.

He decided to walk to the corner shop, not that one, the one owned by the undiluted Cartwrights. He strolls towards the shop (which counts towards his recommended thirty minutes of exercise a day). As he dodges the hopscotch of dog mess he realises that not one person among those he passes is a real man. The women are inevitably womanly... but not one man is specimen enough to be considered.

The first he passes is small, lean like a whippet but soft like a peach, preened to within an inch of his life and brighter than a 'check engine' sign on a good old British made Robin Reliant. What is it? Not a man, definitely.

The next looks a little more worthy of the title. A good, virile beard. A lumberjack. Man's man. Tattoos down one arm yet also on his neck, maybe a sailor, but with cropped hair on one side and tousled on the other? Braces like men used to wear, but matched with piercings like a prize bull and legs you'd find in a woman's exercising magazine. What is it? Not a man.

The third is far more of a man. Excellent posture. Lean but not thin, broad but not wide, but slightly too blond to be British, and too tall actually, carrying a Toblerone... Bloody Swiss? No, can't be, no watch. Scandinavian or some nonsense. Probably stinks of fish and snow. Either way, a foreigner. Not a British man's man.

The fourth performs an act of men! At last, chivalry! A knight's definition of men, opening a door for a lady. Sir Walter Raleigh amongst the natives. A Gentleman... struggling slightly with the weight of the door, but it may be heavy, let's not judge. But what now, taking an earful? From a woman? A scolding no less... for opening a door for her? She can open her own doors? Can she now? He's already struggling with it as it is. Oh, a hung head.

Sign of failure. Pathetic example of a man. Emasculated by a woman. By a feminist of all people. Hairy and braless and angry about everything. Or is that lesbians? He forgets the difference. Aren't they all? Unbelievable. Which is he allowed to say? He shouldn't have to care about such things. He's a man's man. The only man's man for miles.

Here's another feminist strutting about like a braless peacock. No, she is actually dressed as a peacock. Are they pyjamas? Who walks around in pyjamas? Peacock pyjamas only draws more attention to the fact that she's a braless feminist, out in public, charging with determination. To where? The shops, to buy whatever they read. *The Guardian* undoubtedly. Or *Feminist Rag Weekly*. Unbelievable. And another in pyjamas. At least this one is all in black. An all-in-one, whatever they're called, Onesie. Simplistic Americanised name for an adult romper suit. Hideous. And what is she meant to be? Another animal? A gorilla of all things. Can barely see her face. Ah, of course, a hood with ears for full effect.

A policeman! Good, maybe he'll stop her and explain the decency laws. No. Oh, right, obviously being completely covered up as a gorilla is fair game now then. And another one, all in black again, covered head to toe. Less furry though and no ears on the hood, only eyes showing... oh. He's not a racist but there's no difference and a huge difference in what you can and can't say about what they're both wearing and neither are being stopped by the police so he'll back up his right to be politically incorrect by denying he's racist but highlighting his racism.

But the police *are* stopping her? Good. But why is he only stopping one and not the other? Is it body language? The gorilla was walking far more aggressively than this one and her bralessness was far more offensive. But at least they're enforcing something. Again, he's not racist but if the police are stopping and searching them then they're obviously criminals and need to be arrested. Good old bobby on the beat.

'Unbelievable,' said a little girl in bunches with heart sunglasses licking a red lollypop. 'Don't know how they get away with it.'

'I know— Get away with what?' our man asks.

'I don't know, something my mother always says when she sees them.'

'Sees who?'

'Them lot,' she asks, looking up at him, 'are they the good guys?'

'Which ones are you talking about? Nevermind, you wouldn't understand. Someone will tell you when you're old enough to make decisions. And to vote. Can you vote yet? Don't vote. It's bad for you and good for them. And don't stand too close to me.'

'Why?'

'Because I've got a beard and people will see me with a little girl and think I'm a paedophile'

'Why?'

'Because that's how it works.'

'What's a paedo...'

'Argh, off with you!' He shoos her away.

He's not a DJ or TV presenter. Can't be too careful with kids these days. They're everywhere. Looking older and older every day. What's a man to do?

The little girl crosses the street, her little polka dot dress bobbing as she runs across the road without looking...!

Now that's a man! A hero! Saving a little girl from oncoming traffic by dropping his shovel to dive across the road. Superman! Our man rushes over to congratulate the superman.

'That was incredible!' he exclaims, shaking his hand vigorously. 'You're a hero, you should be commemorated and congratulated. Where are the papers when you need them?'

'Sanqueue. I onlee to heilp leetle gorl.' He pushes the words out one by one.

The man raises an eyebrow, 'Not from around here then, are you?'

'No. Poland, I work een houses.' He points across the road to the new housing site.

'What?! In the old site they're finally building on? I've been waiting years for them to start building on there.' He eyes the Pole up and down. 'How did you take that job then?'

'I go to office to ask.'

'Oh, like that is it? Sneaky little tricks of the trade. Do you know how long I've been waiting for them to ask me to work for them?'

The Pole's smile is fixed while his eyes look for clues.

'Coming over here like you own the place and taking our jobs. I bet you're going to move into them houses when they finish ain't you and claim all the benefits you can get your hands on.'

The little girl leaves them both as our man begins to pace back and forth gesticulating wildly. The police van door opens and a moustache in a constable's hat emerges.

'Is there a problem here, gentlemen?' asks the policeman.

'Ah, officer, I'm glad you're here. This man has stolen from me.'

The policeman grabs the Pole's arm. 'What has he stolen, sir?'

'A job I've been waiting for,' our man says, before adding, 'and now he's trying to be a hero by grabbing little girls away from cars.'

'Is this true, sir?' the policeman asks, turning to the Pole.

'Yes. I heilp,' the Pole smiles and nods.

'Right. I'm arresting you on employment theft and attempted pedophilia through a fraudulent act of heroism.' The policeman puts both the Pole's hands behind his back and handcuffs him.

'Ai em nwt paedophiler! Not a filer! Not office man! Building man! I make buildings, please! I have paper and passport!' he pleads.

'And as you can hear, he's not even a homegrown paedophile either!' our man chips in.

'This way, sir. Anything you say will be dismissed as no one can understand you and you're basically a convicted foreign paedophile now.'

A photographer and journalist appear from behind an EU funding street sign. The photographer takes several pictures.

'No pictures! Smile... oops, mind your head there, sir.' The policeman closes the door of the van behind him, lights a pipe and leans against the bonnet. 'There will be no comment from myself or the foreign paedophile at this time.'

'Well this is what I'm talking about,' says our man. 'Good old-fashioned policing. And what about her over there?' He points at the woman in the gorilla suit. 'Aren't you going to arrest her?'

'On what charge, sir? There's no law against wearing costumes.' The policeman puffs out a plume of smoke.

'Well... what about that other one then?' our man exclaims, pointing after her.

'Quite right, sir,' says the policeman, tapping out his pipe. 'How didn't we notice earlier?'

'Weeell, exactly. How didn't you? I'm no officer but I know which people to arrest and which not to. Common Sense.'

The policeman reaches for his radio. 'This is P10D, requesting female assistance for the arrest of an obviously suspicious character, over.'

'What's this guff?' our man says, standing with his hands on his hips. 'Why can't you do it? You don't know who's under there. Might not even be a woman. Look at the height. Could be a man, for all we know. You don't need a woman policeman for that, surely?' He turns to the phototgrapher. 'Couldn't you get one of those upskirt shots like those Pop harlots, so we can have some justice here?'

'Naw, mate, we're current affairs not entertainment,' says the photographer before receiving a text which reads 'Will and Kate curtains. Drop everything. Richmond', hailing an Uber and speeding off.

The policeman clicks his radio again. 'No need for assistance, over.' The policeman walks towards the other woman, opening up a second pair of handcuffs.

'Ah ha! Common sense prevails! I must say, this is excellent stuff. Exactly the type of thing I've come to expect from our police force. Great work. Who's your Police and Crime Commissioner?'

'How should I know?' answers the policeman.

The shop door opens as the policeman handcuffs the woman.

The little girl appears at our man's side again wearing a short skirt and a strap top. 'What happening? This PC gone mad?' she asks.

'Ho ho, very good. No just good old-fashioned police work.' Our man rocks on his heels, smiling holding imaginary lapels to his chest. 'What have you got there?!' He gestures to something she holds in her hand.

The little girl has finished her lollypop and now has a gun with a small price tag tied around the handle. 'My nana gave me some money for helping her with her hot spoon injections and said to buy something nice with it, so I bought some new clothes and this gloc. Isn't it pretty and shiny?'

'Why on earth would you want to buy a gun?!'

'For protection from immigrants and paedophiles, obviously.'

'Oh, yes,' he nods approvingly. 'You've got to watch them lot.'

'Will you walk me across the road, please mister. I was attacked the last time I tried to do it on my own.' She swishes her skirt from side to side and looks up at him, doe-eyed.

'You've got a gun now, what do you need me for—?'

'Pwease?' She flutters her eyelashes and plays with one of her shoulder straps.

'Officer! Officer!' our man screams.

The policeman rushes over from securing the two in the back of the van.

'What seems to be the problem, sir?'

'This little girl is trying to seduce me! Could you please get her away from me by walking her across the road?'

'Could you explain that again please, sir?' the policeman asks, folding his arms.

'This is the girl that Polish paedophile attacked. She asked me to hold her hand to cross the road and when I said no, she rolled that strap on her arm down and fluttered her big beautiful eyelashes at me. Do you know what?' He leans in to whisper, 'I think that man may have been lead on.'

'I'm afraid that matter's closed, sir.' The policeman narrows his eyes. 'Young lady, is this man bothering you at all?'

'No Mr Policeman, he's a nice man. We were walking together earlier.' She smiles.

'No we weren't!' our man protests.

The policeman looks our man square in the face. 'Hmm...' He holds his hand out for the little girl to take. They look both ways before crossing, the policeman glances back at our man who smiles nervously.

On the other side of the road the little girl tugs the policeman's sleeve and whispers something in his ear. He stands and begins crossing the road back towards our man, just as loud sirens wail and screech around the corner, running the policeman over, killing him instantly.

The police van's window rolls down and a bespectacled policeman looks over the edge of the car door. 'Who have I knocked over?' he asks.

175

'A policeman,' answers the man.

'Damn! What type?'

'A constable.'

'No, Not what rank. What type?'

'A local one?'

'Not from where. What type?'

'A white one?'

'Not what colour. What type?'

'An honest one?'

'Aw, that's a shame, a bloody shame. Give his family this when you see them.' He hands the man a card before driving off.

The card reads:

You or your family member
have been a casualty of Her Majesty's Police Force.
Please refer any queries to the
Independent Police Complaints Commission.

'Well, that is efficient,' says our man. He looks up from reading the card and sees the little girl on the other side of the road, now in a bikini, pointing the gun at him. He screams and drops the card as he raises his hands.

'Look what you've gone and made me do?' she shouts.

'What are you talking about, little girl?' he shouts back.

'I'm not a little girl anymore, not after what I've been exposed to. Did you get my text?'

'What?!' squeals our man.

'The text I sent you! God. Check your phone.'

The man fetches a phone from his pocket and sees he has an unread message. He swipes the screen and a banner pops up:

You are about to view images that must only be viewed if you are 18 or over.
Do you agree to the terms and conditions?

The man clicks yes and the image begins to load slowly. '3G signal is dreadful here. They should really do something about it. Bloody EU.' He holds up the phone around him, until a delivery sound clicks. 'Ah, here we go.'

An image of the little girl appears, topless holding a gun.

'Jesus Christ!' screams our man.

A muffled 'Allahu Akbar' comes from the police van.

'Why the bloody hell are you sending me that? What are you thinking?!'

'Did you read the terms and conditions?' the girl asks, still pointing the gun.

'Yes.'

'You read the *whole* terms and conditions and agreed to them?' she asks again.

'Well... no one ever really reads the terms and conditions do they?' He replies sheepishly.

'You should have read the terms and conditions.' She smiles and shoots him in the left leg.

'AAAAAAAAGGGGHHHHH!' Our man falls to the ground screaming and writhing in agony, holding his shattered leg.

'You need to change your settings if you want to keep your other leg intact.'

'GNNNUUUAAAAAAGGGGHHHHH! I hate changing my settings. I like them as they are. This is like the Facebook news feed all over again!'

The girl points the gun at his other leg.

'Oh bloody hell, fine! How do I change that, now?!' Asks the man.

'Just open the image again.'

The man swipes to the image again but another banner appears:

Login details required.

'It's asking for login details...' he exclaims loudly.

She lowers the gun. 'Didn't you login before viewing the image?'

'No.'

'Oh.'

'What do you mean, "Oh"?' asks our man, trying to sit upright.

'I thought you were a member?'

'Of what?'

'The Paedophile Information Exchange—' The girl turns away and quickly checks something on her phone. 'Oh no, this has been a big misunderstanding'. She pulls a blouse, pencil skirt and matching blazer from her backpack and puts them on. She ties her hair back in a bun.

'What do you mean, a misunderstanding?' the man asks between grunts of pain.

'Like an accident at work, this shouldn't have happened to you. Even if you did agree to the terms and conditions, you should only have received the image if you had a valid login account.'

'Am I liable for compensation?' He perks up.

'I'm afraid I cannot confirm nor deny that. What I can say is that you should not have been able to access the images on your phone.'

'It isn't my phone, it's my wife's phone. I only use it to go to the shops in case she needs me to pick up anything else with her papers, fags and luxury tampons.'

'Your wife's phone?'

'She uses it for internet stuff, because I don't trust her with the laptop. Privacy laws and that. Can't trust anyone...' the man says, beginning to speak slower from loss of blood. His wife's face appears before him through a fog of agony, before he realises that it's not his wife's face but the peanut-clad woman that is slowly revealed on the wall of his local pub. The man checks his pockets, he finds and unfolds a photograph of a thin man with a moustache in a suit next to a short squat lady in a white dress with a blonde perm cutting a cake. He strokes the picture and hands it to the girl.

'That's her on the left.'

'You look different now,' says the girl.

'That's not me. That's her ex-husband. Terrible man. Works for the *Observer*.' The man pinches the bridge of his nose and grips his thigh.

'So she could have been a member?' asks the girl.

'What was the original question?' he slurs.

'Could your wife have been a member of the Paedophile Information Exchange?'

Our man remembered his wife's insistence that they put up her signed poster of her membership certificate to a cartooning club in the bedroom. 'Now you mention it...'

'She must have been an original member of PIE.'

'A female paedophile? Don't be so stupid. She can't grow a beard, doesn't wear round glasses and never asked anyone to fix anything for her.'

'Is she a politician?'

'Not that I know of.'

'Worked for the BBC?'

179

'Only briefly during the 60s and 70s, and only ever with DJs or TV presenters. Nothing exciting, just hospital visits and guest house sleepovers and that.'

'Good, then we'll be arresting her this afternoon. You'll need to fill out these forms?'

'What are these for?'

'To exonerate you from any damages, liabilities and/or wrongdoings in relation to the use of mobile phones, online content or firearm incidents.'

Our man scribbles his signature. 'Will I be covered for a courtesy knee?' he says, trying to wipe drool away from his chin.

'No, but you will be allowed to sleep on the streets while we confiscate your possessions and charge your wife.'

'What?!'

'Now, sir, you're a strong man, it's all the rage. Many people become homeless as a lifestyle choice these days, you know.'

'Being homeless isn't a choice! It used to be banned, in the good old days, but now they've legalised it. Two homeless people can even get married now. Unbelievable.'

'No, sir, I believe you're thinking of homosexuals...'

'Oh, what a relief. So I won't have to marry any of them while my wife's away having chemical castration?' He smiles, slipping into delirium. 'That makes sleeping on the streets far more attractive.' He lies down with his head on the pavement.

'Very good, sir, sign here and here and we'll get out of your hair.' The girl folds over the pages of a contract the size of a Quran and points to each section. Holding a pen limply in his hands, our man is guided along by the girl. 'We do apologise for the misunderstanding,' she says.

'So what's going to happen to my wife?'

'I'm afraid the terms and conditions only covers the first party, which is you. And the document you just signed binds us to a non-disclosure agreement so I cannot specify the details.'

'Are we on speaking terms?'

'I'm afraid not. You'll only be allowed to communicate through social media statuses and tagging.'

'Tagging like ankle bracelets or like photographs?' he asks with his eyes closed. 'What about selfies?'

'Selfies are a given, sir. They are a basic human right, like Wi-Fi or being allowed to edit Wikipedia pages,' she says stroking his head.

'Can I send her one before you go?'

'Of course, sir.'

He picks up his phone and sends a selfie:

Bin shot cz of ur old kiddie fiddling login details.LOL.Feel like I'm #dying.FML xx

The man dies clutching his phone, bleeding in the gutter, having signed his life away to an analogy between satire and futurism.

NOTE: This story is regurgitated with words from *Daily Mail*, *Daily Express* and *The Sun* articles and edited with local UKIP, BNP and Britain First leaflets.

The Miller

I bashed the pouring snout with the mallet and the grain began flowing smooth. I stamped hard on the floor and the mill started going again, slow like them old spinning clocks grannies used to get free when they turned sixty-five and joined funeral insurance, when they chose that or a posh pen or some bollocks. Bet none of them would have chosen a clock if they'd have known.

I waited five to check the snout didn't cough again and the stream of flour stayed tidy before shutting the door and heading back to the house. I put the padlock on hard and whacked it to make sure.

ALWAYS CHECK THE PADLOCK.

It weren't smelling half bad when I opened the kitchen door, wafting warm and nostalgic... but, I don't know... tainted.

'Moira, that smells like...'

'Cawl, it is,' she said.

'Aye, but there's obviously summin' in it...'

'Course there is,' she said. 'Meg copped it.'

'What?!'

'Meg. She copped it s'morning.'

'How the fuck didn't I know about that?!' I said.

''Cause you were fiddling about next door, like you always do, is why!'

'Fiddling about? Fiddlin... That's the fucking mill, mun!'

'Alright, alright, stop swearing,' she said trying to simmer us down. 'She copped it. We're eating tidy because of it. Don't matter now, do it? Plus, I seen your eyes go all Bopa Colwill when you smelt it.'

She was right. Smelled exactly like Bopa Colwill's cawl, stew, whatever you want to call it.

'Except she used lamb obviously...' She stirred the pot, stared out the window. I don't know if she gave a shit about Meg. She was a hard woman, Moira, but I know she still struggled every now and again. She wouldn't cry about it or nothing but it'd still be bloody horrible to chop your own dog up... again. She kicked the buggery out the dresser last time 'cause I refused to do it.

'It's your dog!' I said.

'Don't care, I ain't doing it!'

Mabli she was called. Lovely nature but sickly. She couldn't hack it like the rest of the dogs after it happened. Each of them went a bit funny but she was all over the shop for a bit, barking at nothing, whimpering all the time. I found her sitting in the stream once, on the bad side and then she just started falling apart. Poor bugger. We got home one day and she must have got into the house somehow. I was about to go ape and drag her out when we realised she was gone. She was curled up under the cooker (ironically), dead as fuck. We argued for a while 'bout it but fair do's to Moira, she could just switch off. She did the same with her father. Accept the death and then do what's necessary.

'Chuck me that bloody cleaver!' she said. 'I won't have her looking at me while I'm doing it,' and then she just went and chopped Mabli's head off and flung it at me.

Without having a chance to react properly I volleyed it. It rolled across the kitchen floor and came to a stop by my boots, looking back at me. Didn't seem right to pick it up and hold her head like I used to do, *cwtched* up by the fire. So I had to punt it out into the yard.

'Don't do that!' said Moira. 'Whack it on a spike and chuck it up by the top stream so them Lungcats don't go trouting again.'

Hard woman, she is, Moira, but a good girl. Course if I told her that she'd cut my balls off for being so soft.

'Get over it, mun, Gray,' she said turning back from the window.

'I will as soon as I get a bowl in me,' I said fetching the crockery out of the cupboard and putting them either side of the big oak table.

'Where's the spoons to?' I asked, checking through the cutlery drawer.

'By the laptop, by there, look,' she nodded to the chair under the stairs.

'Why do you keep using the spoons instead of them tools I gave you?' I asked. 'They're precision tools especially for fiddling with computers.'

''Cause a spoon does a better job wedging under the battery plate,' she said. 'We need an upgrade. That's starting to play up all the bloody time now.' She looked over at me.

'I ain't going riffling and nicking,' I said.

'You've been down there plenty now. There's definitely a gig or two you can swipe with no one seeing. What do them mankin' morons want 'em for anyway?'

'We're honest,' I said.

'Honest, be buggered! There ain't no honest now!'

'Well we still are!' I thumped the table, knowing she only starts this argument to hear me say it. She stood quiet for a while staring out the window again.

'The only bloody ones...' she muttered.

'Fuckin' A!!' I said to enforce it. To separate us from them. The good and the bad. We're the goodies. They're the baddies.

The laptop is on its last legs, mind. Only so much solar power that panel's going to hold before it packs in and all. Only portable it is. Should have taken that deal when that bellend came round selling them. Gave us that little one as a trial while we 'thought about it' and then he said he'd bring the big mounted solar panel rig to show us, when he came back. That'd have saved us a shitload of hassle if we had bought it. Course he never came back. No one did.

We're sustainable as hell up here but a full-on rig could have kept us going for years before we... I had to start finding new ways around it. The mill's a good source but there's only so much wind and water. Moira never liked it much anyway, so it don't play on her to think how it keeps going when there ain't no wind or when the stream's only a trickle. What I've had to do to keep it going so long. To be honest, I don't even know what the fuck she would do if she knew, considering...

We keep to ourselves but people find out. They come across a windmill in the middle of nowhere, they're gonna start nosing. Eventually they're gonna try something. They were bound to. They must have seen me in the field. Just a stupid old miller plodding along while the rest of the world burned. But I weren't always a miller and I ain't fuckin' stupid neither. Jealousy, anger, hunger, whatever they were feeling when they tried to get in, they saw an opportunity. But never underestimate a man that looks as if he's got fuck all to fight with, especially when he's got everything to fight for. You can only push a man so far. But you can make a man, two men in fact, push for as long as you want, so long as you got food, water and a big fuckin' stick. So the mill keeps turning...

It wasn't like we picked what we were and weren't going to do. I knew how to work a mill from working with my uncle at the folk museum and I thought she could help out, little jobs, while I done the lumping about and the farming. I just wanted to keep us going with enough to eat and up here, out of the way, out of the towns, was safer than anywhere else I could think of.

You can see clean straight down the lane from the corner of the yard, all the way to the cattle grid before the upturned oak lying across it. That storm was a blessing. I couldn't have built a better barricade. Then it's a good ten – twelve miles to the nearest anything. The stream comes straight out of the top field so it don't get much cleaner. Nothing to spoil it. The other stream on the south side, mind, down the slag heaps is a different bag of Smarties. Passes through the old coal tips, full of rusting bits of tram and rail lines and what have you. Right in the middle, that pipe comes out of the ground, oozing whatever's left after coughing up years of industry and death. After all this time, I still don't understand how it can have any shit left to come out. Whatever's inside rotting needs to find a way out I s'pose. But I ain't going anywhere near it to find out.

Our two fields are far enough up here that the wind don't carry nothing. Even if it does or if it ever *has* carried anything, in seven years nothing's come of it. Wind carries whatever it wants, but it always blows down towards the towns, away from us.

So I mill and farm the wheat. Moira keeps the house in good nick, does the veg in the garden and watches the lane. The veg is right in front of the house just below the kitchen window so no matter what she's doing in or out of the house, she can still watch the lane.

ALWAYS WATCH THE LANE.

Like I said, we never picked what we were or weren't going to do. I'm a big enough workhorse who can carry most of what needs carrying. She makes a cracking loaf, can fiddle with the tech stuff and she can shoot a hole through the eye of any fucker who tries coming up the lane without us knowing.

Lungcats she calls them, since they can't breathe tidy by the time they reach us and she don't trust a single one of them. She only speaks to the ones that can breathe. If they can breathe tidy then they ain't a Lungcat, which means they ain't from the towns, which means they don't do what Lungcats do, which Moira ain't partial to and more fool them if they come close enough to try to change her mind. Not after last time. Fool her once, shame on her, but fool her twice and you'll have half your mush shot off.

Last time she let them come too close, I was up in the field and that was the first and only time she buggered up. She stayed in bed two weeks 'cause of that, messed her up.

He came up the lane calling her name, which no one ever did. No one knew us and we knew no one left. We didn't need to know no one. He came slowly up the lane, purposefully towards the mill, calling her name, but more like a moaning wail. It was horrible. I remember running down from the field when I heard it 'cause it didn't sound like anything good. It sounded like a warning. It sounded like mistakes.

I came over the side of the field where I could see the roof of the house and the lane beyond it. This Lungcat was walking with his arms out, like a child longing for a mother. They all did that. I knew that, but I must never have told Moira. They all walk like that towards you 'cause they all want you to help them. They think that you can help and that you'll have a cure or an answer or an end.

He was past the fence line and I was thinking, fuck, something must have happened, she hasn't seen him. Then I heard the shot and he fell to the ground like a sack of shit and that awful sound stopped. The shot rang out for a while, dancing around the mill. But he got near enough to her and she saw what can happen when you got caught in it.

When I went to the towns, what I saw there, I told her about. I'd tell her that it was nothin' like the films we used to watch on Saturday nights *cwtched* up on the sofa. Films where no matter how far into the future it was, no matter how much of a dystopia, there was still rubbish and newspapers strewn everywhere and everyone had a gun. Bollocks. There is no rubbish because nobody has anything to throw away. If they do, it's worth something, so they can trade. Nobody leaves anything lying around. Paper is a rarity and if you've got a gun, you don't tell anyone. 'Cause then all the other fuckers with a gun will try to put an hole in you before you can even shit yourself. *That* part is like the videos we watched.

But the destitution, poverty and sickness? Nobody could have dreamed of making a film that even came close. I'd tell her about their faces and skin and about their hair and eyes. I'd tell her that those that ain't fucked up wrap scarves around their faces. Healthy faces are covered up. They still think you can catch it. But those of us that know it ain't an airborne virus keep our faces covered so we can make sure we can see. So we can make sure we can see *them* coming and make sure that they never touch us.

But the people in the towns, they were all strangers to Moira. They were details about places she didn't want to visit. They were horror stories to keep her staying safe up here by knowing that it weren't safe down there. Stories full of Lungcats, deformed, horrific victims turned dangerous, scarred scavengers. They weren't family. They weren't her flesh and blood. They weren't her brother who had heard that she lived by a mill in the mountains and had come for help, but who couldn't breathe tidy and who was too deformed to be recognised from that distance, but came close enough to get his jaw blown off. They weren't the one she buried.

A sister shot a brother in the head because she knew that he was not what he once was. The same as a daughter had to do when she first learned these things. When she saw the changes. The slow ravaging. The laboured breathing, the wheezing confusion, the buckled hands unable to hold, unwilling to touch, mercy folded. A father would have to die for a daughter to live. But he was not her father. Not on that day.

Learning and understanding are two very different things.

A mother would see a smoking gun resting against the pantry door. She would see a daughter sitting alone in the garden staring across at the new and confused purple skies. She would see a crimson pool halo what was once a father, lying on the living room floor. She would see and understand one thing, that a daughter would learn from this new world while a mother never would. She would understand the simple differences. Before and after, past and future, living and dying, loaded and unloaded. Learning would require far more than understanding. Learning would require many things, while understanding would require only one.

So many single shots rang out in those early days.

Families are memories. They were Things That Happened. You either clung to them or were killed by them. We forced ourselves to forget. That's why we were up here away from everything. Down there you might see someone you thought you knew before. But they weren't those people anymore. They were never going to be the same people after what happened. But if you wavered, if you thought, I know this person, this person was my friend once, this is somebody I used to love, this is somebody I should help. I should look after this person because that's who we are. A help in hand, a stroke of a cheek, a loving squeeze. One compassionate touch would be enough to do it. If you thought like this then it wouldn't be long before you were wandering up a lane, with your arms out like a child, wailing and moaning through your deformed windpipe because you couldn't speak but wanted, like nothing else on this ruined earth, to be comforted and loved again. But we are not what we used to be and he was not her brother. Not on that day.

The Things That Happened happened and now these are the things that must be done to avoid them happening again.

Two days in bed she had.

Like I said, hard woman, Moira is.

Treiglad/Mutation

I

Iaith sy'n rhan nid iaith sy'n rhaid.
Iaith ŵyr ac wyres o famgu a thaid.
Nid iaith lwyd ond bwyd
a gwaed a thraed
i gerdded allan o orfodiaith
o'r daith frwydro,
nid iaith a grwydrodd i fae Caerdydd
ar dafod gwleidyddion
a throi iaith y werin yn ddeddf,
troi gwreiddiau cryf
yn gaeth i gyfieithu
ar bapur, arwyddion, adroddiadau,
ac yn amlwg nawr yn y gwallau
yn ngwaith cartref cenedl
â thrwydded i Google translate,
ond nid i 'talko wrth y school gate'.
A'r eironi fel mae'r iaith yn newid
o'r gâd i'r gât,
cyfieithiad 'mutation' yw 'treiglad'.
Wrth anwybyddu'r dealltwriaeth hwn
trwy wynebau syn â bysedd mewn clust,
mae'r gorfodaeth yn magu'r esgeulus

gan feio dysgwyr am y Saesnegyddol
(y genedl gyferbyn)
ac erbyn i ni ddeall hyn
prin fydd dim ar ôl ond
y 'Welsh Must',
y 'Rhaid Cymraeg'.

II

Ymarferiad yn casglu llwch
tu ôl i'n llyfrau hanes,
yn dal i ddysgu dim ohonynt,
Mond brawddegau hurt anobeithiol
wedi'u dethol gan eiriadur a llond ceg
ar ran tegwch
ond nid dealltwriaeth.
Gofyniad cenedlaethol,
yn troi llygaid darllenwyr yn llaethog.
Penderfyniad wedi'i ethol ganddom ni, y bobol,
trwy donnau'n teithio'n Ogleddol,
Ar lan y môr mae 'Nghaerdydd innau
(i fod)
Sy'n penderfynu dyfodol fy nhafod
ond mae gofod rhwng y ddau,
sy'n cael ei lenwi gan eiriau gwag
gwleidyddion âg atgofion, gofidion

a thraed mewn cyffion,

bygythion o amser maith yn ôl

cyn glo a Charlo ac S4C.

Cyn i arglwyddi a brenhinoedd gario clecs

gyda llythyr neu aderyn.

Y werin yn defnyddio iaith

o drafodaeth a chân.

Eu dŵr a thân.

Wrth fyw a marw,

Cyn i Grist o'r Nef cael ei bregethu

mewn Lladin, hwn fu bron aberthu

arweiniaeth dros weriniaeth

mewn gwlad wyllt heb reolaeth.

Arglwyddi Brycheiniog, Morgannwg, Meirionnydd

Dan reolaeth Tudur mewn gwirionedd.

Trwy ddatrys problem ei mawrhydi,

Elizabeth lwyddodd i gomisiynnu,

yr esgob William Morgan i glymu

Iaith a chrefydd i'r bobol foli,

ac osgoi'r gwîr ddatganoli.

Achub cenedl trwy fod yn blwyfol

Collwyd coron ond yr iaith yn llwyddo.

Braidd bum can mlynedd ers cyfieithu'r Gair,

Rydym dal yn gaeth i'r un Arglwyddi.

III

Nid atom ni rhaid anelu'r ornest,
Ond at wasanaethwyr y frenhines,
Yr un un enw, yr un cymdogion
i ddanfon datganiad ei gweinidogion.

Y presennol, prin sydd wedi newid
rhain sydd dal i beri gofid.
Coch neu las neu wyrdd neu felyn,
pob plaid am eu bara menyn
yn bygwth newid, byth gair o wir
'mond pellter y daith a'u darn o dir.
Ond cyn bo hir clywn ganu'r gloch
lle bu dannedd cynddeiriog yn brathu'r foch
i ddenu gwaed, i godi cywilydd
am ddiffyg parch tuag at ein gilydd,
cyn colli popeth mewn araith a ffin
mewn pŵer gormes yn ein geiriau ein hunain.
'Adeiniog pob chwant'
ond methiant ydyw
heb ddealltwriaeth o golled Cernyw,
heb ddysgu dim ond gorfoleddu
ein bod yn genedl falch o fod yn Gymry?
Ond balchder am falchder y boblogaeth
am ddarn o dir dan sail,'Y Dywysogaeth'?

Buasai'n ddigon i ymladd pe bai Carlo'n gofyn?
Neu fydd cleddyfau yn cwympo ymhysg y chwerthin?
Mae'r nod yn glîr ond ma'r coesau'n baglu

os y gwelwn fel rhywbeth sy'n araf bydru.
Cheith be mae Cymru angen fyth ei ganiatáu,
os yw bod yn flaengar yn cael ei trin fel angau.

IV
Hen gred o frwydro dros rywbeth,
Nid dim ond tîr, ond rhywbeth clir
Nid Pontcanna yw canolbwynt y wlad
A ni fydd Gwynedd yn cael ei gwerthu yn rhad,
heb gysylltu'r De a'r Gogleddol
beth yw'r gobaith am ein dyfodol?
Rhaid uno'r bobol, yr ieithoedd, y cyfan
neu parhau cael ein bwydo o San Steffan
Dros y bont i ddoc Penfro
O Fôn i Fynwy unwaith 'to.
O gopa'r Wyddfa i lawr i'r traethau

Mae'r wlad hon yn fuddsoddiad ganddyn nhw i ni!
Mae digon gennym i ddarlledu
o dan lygaid barcud y BBC
'rhodd' i'r genedl er dicter Maggie

a'n amod ni fydd mwy o lwgu,
er degawdau o newynu
gadawodd yn ei sgil ers hynny.
Ond a oes digon nawr i dyfu?
I greu, i fagu, i ddirgrynnu
Trwy gnawd cenhedlaeth Cymru gyfan
heb dennyn byr a thyn San Steffan.
Heb fewnfrwydro eto am ba lwybr a heol,
heb greu dyrchafiad yn ddeddf a rheol,
I'r jac, y Cardi, y gogs, yr hwntws,
y ddau draw fyna ac y 'you two's'
y twpsyn, myfyriwr, y werin, y crach,
yr hud a lledrith, y dewin, y wrach,
y capel, yr eglwys, y beirdd, unawdwyr,
y bêl hirgron, y ffwtbol, yr awdur,
yr Eisteddfod, Glan Llyn, Llangrannog,
y cwmwl, y glaw, yr heulwen a'r cysgod.
Nid 'Duw a ŵyr' ond ni sy'n dewis,
rhaid codi llaw a thorchi llewys,
Gallwch anwybyddu annibyniaeth
Heb ddeall bod dyfodol mewn dwy iaith.
Amser maith yn ôl ac amser pell ymlaen.
Angor da yw gobaith
ond dealltwriaeth yw'n hadain.
Nid blwch bleidleisio oedd y 'Mimosa,'

A ni ddaw'r gorwel yn agosach,
swyddogaeth Bae yw i lanio, i fesur, i ddocio,
rhaid deall rhyddid cyn i'r tennyn lacio,
Cyn ceisio cyfarth am atebion
rhaid gweld y ddwy iaith fel un par o olion,
un tafod yn gofyn, Ni'r Cymry sy'n gwybod,
nid inc ar bapur na llinell yn y tywod.

Treiglad/Mutation

I

A language for, not forced
from parent to grandchild, Mamgu & Taid.
Not a grey language,
but the blood and sand
which blooms from the oppression
that once hung around our neck.
Not one that wandered into Cardiff Bay
on a politician's tongue
to turn the people's language into laws –
the roots of a nation
now slaves to translation –
on paper, signs and reports,
and from homework in a state,
with a debt owed to Google Translate,
but not to 'Siarad at the school gate'...
yet there's irony
in where the battle begins.
From shawl to school to street to state,
in *Cymraeg*, to change is to 'mutate'.
Ignorance is bliss for an agenda
with its fingers in its ears,
persisting with insistence

breeds negligence and blame
while learning leads to Anglicise
from failure and from shame,
and by the time we realise
if there's turning in the tide
there'll be nothing left
but the 'Welsh Must',
Y 'Rhaid Gymraeg'.

II
A Practice collecting dust
on the shelves of History
that we still learn nothing from,
but absurdly wordy sentences
selected by a dictionary
a National expectancy
with a propensity for *penbleth*,
a decision elected by representatives
creating waves flowing north.
From CF99, the route is long,
deciding the future of our mother tongue,
but the void between north and south
fills with words from empty mouths.
Politicians remind us of the pains
of a judiciary with its feet in chains.

To hide the threat of memory
before coal and Charles and S4C.
Before lords and kings
passing letters to seal the fates
of the clans who spoke and sang,
who lived and died
in their own language.
It fed their fire, it was their water.
Before Christ Almighty found his way in
with fire and brimstone and Latin.
Barely five hundred years since QE1
commissioned Reverend William Morgan
to take The Word for Welsh translation,
'A Gift' that bound us from separation
to devout clandestine subjugation.

III

It isn't inward our ire should stir
but towards the Queen's Westminster.
Still the same name, the same direction,
to control a land from insurrection.
Today the tide is yet to turn
it's them that still cause most concern.
Red or Blue, Yellow, Green
new clans campaign in irony,

promising Change and *chwarae teg*,

elections pass, each one reneges.

But soon the bells will start to sound

and the simmering rage will demand a pound

of flesh for their piecemeal suppression.

Renewed after every fresh election.

Hiding it all in speeches and borders.

Repeated in every government order.

With every vote we remain oppressed.

Misfortune's well is idleness.

But not if the fortune lies idle elsewhere,

flowing one way but not from there.

It means nothing when all our spoils are spoilt,

in our eagerness to prove a point,

claiming victories of sporting prowess,

yet cannot find words to profess

that pride swells in the heart of the Welsh

but pride for pride's sake and nothing else?

How can we claim parity,

when referred to still, as a 'Principality'?

If we were commanded to battle by Charles,

laughter would roar before we took up arms.

like flies against the window pane

trapped, they hope our claims would wane.

What Wales wants isn't on the shelf.

They won't allow us to feed ourselves!

IV

An old belief to fight *for* something,

we need to get this new ball rolling.

The epicentre's NOT Pontcanna.

We can't rely on Gwynedd forever,

without joining the south *and* north

we won't stop dependence dripping forth

from east to west down the M4,

from Parliament to Pembroke Dock.

We hear our voice on our own TVs

but 'bestowed' as a branch of the BBC.

Is it tactical to thwart our growing?

To keep us afloat, for fear of drowning?

Could we swim, reach land and thrive?

Connect, elect, support, survive?

Through the cities, towns and countryside?

A tapestry of many lives;

The Jack, the Port, the Valley boy,

the borders, farmers, hoi polloi,

the Diff, The Westy and the deacon,

the singer, shepherds up on Snowdon,

the *twp*, the sharp, the out of work,

the rugby player, striker, clerk,

the Eisteddfodwr, the silent, the mouth,
the north, east, west and the south,
the sun, the snow, the wind and rain,
the arms, the legs, the heart, the brain.
'God knows' won't cut it any longer
WE, the people, must be stronger.
But Independence without foundation,
won't improve the situation.
The ballot box is no 'Mimosa'.
Horizons don't come any closer.
A Bay is for landing, surveying, to dock,
so, are we to carve Cymru or Wales in the rock?
Before searching for the answers,
(since flags and pride are different anchors)
both tongues' questions must understand,
they're not written in ink nor lines in the sand.

Acknowledgements

Nu: Fiction & Stuff (Parthian, 2009)

Nu 2: Memorable Firsts (Parthian, 2011)

Ten of the Best (Parthian, 2011)

Square Magazine 8 (Square, 2011)

Red Poets 18 (Red Poets, 2011)

Red Poets 20 (Red Poets, 2013)

Cheval 6 (Parthian, 2013)

Planet Magazine 213 (Planet, 2013)

Cheval 7 (Parthian, 2014)

Red Poets 21 (Red Poets, 2014)

When Young Dragons Meet Young Dodos (L'Atelier d'ecriture, 2014)

Cheval 8 (Parthian, 2015)

Red Poets 22 (Red Poets, 2015)

Cheval 9 (Parthian, 2016)

Gigobytes (Coolideer Ltd, 2015)

Wales Arts Review (2016)

Huge thanks should be given to every editor and judge that deemed my work publishable and/or award worthy over the years.

Versions of these stories, poems and essays appeared in these anthologies, magazines and competitions: 'Also Elizabeth' appeared in *Red Poets 18*, 'The Oxymoron' appeared in *Red Poets 21*, an early version of 'Treiglad/Mutation' appeared in *Red Poets 22*. 'Conservatives to Re-open the Mines: A Dialogue' appeared in *Square Magazine 8*. An early version of the story 'Running into the Ground' won the runner-up prize in the Terry Hetherington Award 2013, a version of 'Every Cloud' won the runner-up prize in the Terry Hetherington Award the following year. 'The Poet, The Donkey and The Quandary' won the 'Wales in Hard Times' Young Essay Writers Award in *Planet Magazine 2013*. Elements of 'The stone from which our blood is drawn' was written for National Theatre Wales' Treorchy Assembly in 2013. 'Estate of Mind' was written for Commonwealth Theatre's 'Nationalisation' production on the Gurnos Estate, Merthyr and was Highly Commended in the Welsh Poetry Competition 2014. 'The Miller' appeared in *When Young Dragons Meet Young Dodos* in 2014 in Mauritius and Welsh editions. A version of 'God Bless 'Merica' appeared in *Cheval 8*. The cartoon, 'Geith Gymru Fwy?' appeared on the Golwg360 blog. 'Just like his Father' appeared on Wales Arts Review in 2016.

Cawl was partly funded by an IndieGoGo crowdfunding campaign. The author and publisher would like to thank all those who pledged money to help make it happen.

Thankiws

First of all I thank my wife, who gave me purpose, support, love, our wonderful daughter and tried her best to get me to come to bed early (even though I never did). I write while you sleep so I don't miss a laugh, a smile or moment. My family, *Mam a Dad a Dan* for always fostering every single creative idea I ever had, no matter how daft, and for always being genuinely pleased with my achievements and honest in their opinions. *Caru Chi.* She's not here anymore but without the Munci, much of the inspiration and ideas at the heart of this book wouldn't be. I always said I'd dedicate my first book to her, Dad said it was a nice gesture but she much preferred watching *The Thornbirds* and *Pobol y Cwm* to reading. *Y Gogs, Caru Chi.* Pentre originals, *Caru Chi.* My in-laws, Caryl, Tim, Kirsty (for the pen that wrote the entire book!), Thomas, Kieran, Muriel and co. Loviw and you may not think it, but you're just as mental, which has always been a great comfort.

Susie Wild for telling me every time we met to send stuff in to her and for working hard to edit *Cawl*, being patient with me and for sorting my dreadful grammar. *Diolch mawr i Sian Northey a Siôn Aled* for the editing the bilingual and Welsh poems. Rob for finalising the cover, which made me daft happy to finally see. Richard Lewis Davies, first of all for writing *Work, Sex and Rugby*, a novel which gave me such confidence to write about the hyperlocal and still get published. Secondly, for the conversation on a train from Carmarthen where he gave me a can of Stella and made me think more about writing than *being* a writer. And thirdly, for telling me in a London pub that Parthian would like to publish a collection of my work.

Thanks to Dominic and Tomos, who were the first to see something in an angry valley boy's poetry worthy of publishing in *Nu: fiction & stuff*, an anthology that is quickly becoming the 'Footlights' of the Young Welsh Lit scene, and for introducing me to Mao (Michael Oliver-Semenov) and James Smythe. Mao, who is forever my creative spring-board, my adventurous inspiration and my source of transcontinental Facebook hilarity, you are a gem, butt. James for showing that relentless creativity can be achieved and inspiration can come from Twitter.

Gethin Down for always being willing to read my work and give proper tidy critiques while also laying claim to being my official biographer. Josh Geake and Matt Booker for being my online political sparring partners. Kyle, Jack and Bob for being cracking butties and also for drinkin', talkin' and sparkin' ideas and looking after 'Shenanigans'. The Ynyswen, Cymer, Myrddin 7 massive & Swansea crew for ultimately supplying me with the seeds for my stories and poems. Thank you to inspirational lecturers at Coleg y Drindod – Jenny, Menna, Neil and Paul. Neil Burridge at GCADT who really opened my mind up creatively and injected so much humour and satire into my work. Steeeeeeeeve. Gavin and National Theatre Wales and the Parc and Dare Theatre where some of these poems were written. Nerea Martinez De Lecea for the birds of introduction and the drive to create. Martin Rowson for a conversation at a particular low point last year and a retweet that made me feel like George Bailey. Roald Dahl for writing *Matilda*, which made me want to read and Treorchy Library, where my love of books flourished.

Thank you to every employer that ever made me redundant and for fuelling my pen of rage, particularly YGCR. If you hadn't made me redundant at the time you did, I wouldn't have had that first three months with my daughter or been able to finish this book. In conjunction, *Diolch anferth i Emyr, Osian a Cwmni Da* for saving us during this time. *Newidioch chi bopeth.* You changed my life. Lou and Marilyn Cosy Cafe for the jazz, Everton mints and every description of old ladies I've ever written. Ron and everyone at The Brynffynnon for the idea for 'Every Cloud'. The Fforch for 'The Miller'. Everyone at Ciryl's for 'Cawl'. Treorchy Rugby Club for being a fountain of ridiculously hilarious dialogue, descriptive character features and years of releasing my aggression valve on the Oval. Glyncorrwg for my Meadow Prospect. Heidi for allowing me to use the Instagram shot at the centre of the cover. Delyth Seaton (nee Caffery) for breaking her foot, which forced me to take her sixth form reg class where a lot of this book was typed up.

Thanks too for the support from the Dylan Thomas Centre, Mike Jenkins and the Red Poets, Nick Fisk and *Square*, and everyone at Y Gloran. My greatest thank you is to everyone at the Terry Hetherington Awards and *Cheval*, especially Aida, Alan and Jonathan, whose belief, support, advice and friendship continues to be the foundation of my writing. I am forever indebted to you.

Finally I thank my valley and its people for shaping me from the lumpy ginger clay I was to who I am today. If I was not born and raised in the Rhondda, this book would be non-existent.

I love you to my very core.
Diolch dudwyll.

New Poetry from Parthian

parthianbooks.com